MY LOVE, MY LOVE
OR THE PEASANT GIRL

My Love, My Love,

or The Peasant Girl

by Rosa Guy

COFFEE HOUSE PRESS

MINNEAPOLIS

COFFEE HOUSE PRESS is an independent nonprofit literary publisher supported
in part by a grant provided by the Minnesota State Arts Board, through an
appropriation by the Minnesota State Legislature, and in part by a grant from
the National Endowment for the Arts. Significant support was received for this
project through a grant from the National Endowment for the Arts, a federal
agency, and the Jerome Foundation. Support has also been provided by Athwin
Foundation; the Bush Foundation; Buuck Family Foundation; Elmer L. &
Eleanor J. Andersen Foundation; Honeywell Foundation; James R. Thorpe
Foundation; Laura Jane Musser Fund; Lila Wallace-Reader's Digest Fund;
McKnight Foundation; The Medtronic Foundation, Patrick and Aimee Butler
Family Foundation; Phillips Family Foundation; The St. Paul Companies
Foundation, Inc.; the law firm of Schwegman, Lundberg, Woessner & Kluth,
P.A.; Star Tribune Foundation; Marshall Field's Project Imagine with support
from the Target Foundation; Verizon; Wells Fargo Foundation Minnesota; West
Group; and many individual donors. To you and our many readers across the
country, we send our thanks for your continuing support.

COFFEE HOUSE PRESS books are available to the trade through our primary dis-
tributor, Consortium Book Sales & Distribution, 1045 Westgate Drive, Saint
Paul, MN 55114. For personal orders, catalogs, or other information, write to:
Coffee House Press, 27 North Fourth Street, Suite 400, Minneapolis, MN 55401.

LIBRARY OF CONGRESS CIP INFORMATION

Guy, Rosa.
  My Love, my love, or, The peasant girl / Rosa Guy.
    p. cm
    ISBN-13: 978-1-56689-131-8 (alk. paper)
    ISBN-10: 1-56689-131-0 (alk. paper)
    1. Caribbean Area—Fiction. 2. Social classes—Fiction.
    I. Title: My love, my love. II. Title: Peasant girl. III. Title.

  PS3557.U93 M9 2002
  1813'.54—DC21

                                              2001058250

To Joan Sandler and Marsha Gillespie.

ONE

On that island where rivers run deep, where the sea sparkling in the sun earns it the name Jewel of the Antilles, the tops of the mountains are bare. Ugly scrub brush clings to the sides of their gray stones, giving the peaks a grim aspect that angers the gods and keeps them forever fighting. These terrible battles of the gods affect the lives of all the islanders, rich and poor. But the wealthy in towns, protected from the excesses of the gods' furies, claim to be masters of their own destiny. The peasants accept the will of the gods as theirs. They pray to the gods when times are hard and give thanks to them when life goes well.

But then the peasants live in the valleys and mountain villages amid flamboyants, poinsettias, azaleas, ficus, eucalyptus, and magnolias—their colors raging over the countryside and blending roads into hills, hills into forests. Multicolored flora defy the destructiveness of man and climate to spring eternally back to life. This miracle the peasants attribute to the gods.

On this island of mountains, forests, hills, and valleys is a lovely peasant village. Huts and wooden frame houses cling to the hillside and nestle on the flatlands of the forest. As in most of the poor villages of the island, each hut stands in its own field on a plot of forested land deeded to the peasants at an earlier time. Trees in the woods surrounding each clearing add fruit to the legumes the peasants must cultivate for their survival. It makes for a very meager existence. But to these gentle people it might seem a paradise, were they not always victims of the whims of gods—and man.

"Once upon a time," said Monsieur Bienconnu, the village centenarian, "the mountains of this Jewel of the Antilles were thick with hardwood trees. The hardest in all the world. Trees reached up from the mountaintops to touch the heavens. They excited the senses and challenged the genius of our men.

"Asaka, goddess of earth, of plants, of all growing things, how generous was her bounty then. She pushed a wilderness of herbs, of bush to thicken the underbrush, keeping the trees forever green, forever productive.

"We peasants worshipped her. Our praise of her rang through the valleys, up through the hills, and on to the mountaintops. With our drums, our songs, we gave her thanks. Our well-being was woven into the fabric of abundance. Asaka smiled and we laughed with joy. She laughed and we danced—forever in one fraternal embrace . . ."

M. Bienconnu gazed out over the heads of the old couple and the peasant girl working their field. He stared out, looking back in time.

"Agwe, god of the sea, of our many waters—how gentle he was then. How tenderly he treated the voluptuous Asaka. He adored her. Agwe's caresses nourished the fruits of her work, and rained gently down on us, his benediction, the benediction of the gods."

Mama Euralie and Tonton Julian kept their heads bent over their work. They had been raking through the dry, parched earth since early morning. Now the sun was at its height. They had no patience for the tales of old men, which they knew all too well.

But the peasant girl listened. She stopped her work to gaze up at the mountains. Their bare peaks shone in the bright light of the noonday sun. She imagined them as they had once appeared—fertile, thick with trees, and green—a green that blended them in with the descending hills. Green, green hills, vibrant, intense—a reminder of what this Jewel of the Antilles must once have been.

"Men, men, men, foolish men." M. Bienconnu stood up. The rock on which he had been sitting had once been jagged but was now rubbed smooth, through years of his daily visits. "Foolish men, what disaster they court with their greed. Cutting down our trees—our god-given gifts—and selling them for gain. Stripping Asaka of her riches and giving nothing back. Nothing. Do you wonder that Asaka sulks? Do you wonder that she treats us with indifference? And Agwe, your god of waters—how he punishes her. And what abuse he heaps upon us." The old man moved stiffly across the beaten path to the woods that screened the old couple's plot from that of their neighbors. "Men," he grumbled. "Their greed will be the destruction of us."

Mama Euralie lifted her head, her bright eyes impish in her wrinkled black face. "We peasants, too, need the charcoal that the wood brings to cook our food."

The old man had disappeared through the woods, but his answer floated back. "Oui, oui, they sold their souls for a few pieces of silver. Ours, too."

Tonton Julian waited until M. Bienconnu was well out of hearing. Then he stopped working to say, "Whatever, we need rain now—now." He bent and scooped up a handful of soil. It ran through his fingers like sand. "Another week without rain, and it might well be the end of us poor peasants."

"It will rain soon," Mama Euralie said. She sniffed the air. "A day or so . . . a week at the most, oui. It's on its way."

"Is that your old bones talking?" Tonton Julian asked his wife. "Or did Agwe come and whisper in your ear? If so, how much rain? How little?" He waved her silent with gnarled hands. "Never mind. Too little rain will not help this drought. Too much will wash away the soil. And there you are—your gods making playthings of us poor peasants."

"Mon Dieu, but you blaspheme, Monsieur Julian," the little woman scolded. She looked up at her thin, lanky husband. "Have faith. The gods have never abandoned us yet—neither the gods of our fathers nor the One who rules over them."

"Old woman," Tonton Julian growled, throwing

wide his arms and looking over their parched lot of land. "You see life through eyes already dead."

The peasant girl stopped raking through the sandy soil and smiled. The banter between the old couple amused her. Tonton Julian saw her smiling and smiled too, exposing his two remaining teeth. Then he walked toward his old mule tied to the post behind their mud hut, touching the peasant girl gently on her head as he passed. She followed his movements—his bony thighs that showed through the flapping tear of his ragged pants as he walked, the dry skin of his feet as he swung his long frame onto his mule. She liked the way he adjusted his straw hat to keep the open crown away from the top of his head.

Then she stopped seeing; a car was racing past on the distant road.

She strained, listening to the fading sound of its engine. Her eyes were alert, shining. A car. A car. From what unknown place had it come? To what strange place was it going? Oh, to be flying against the wind in a car. To be rushing off to a city, a town . . .

The old woman sounded a note of warning at the girl's excitement. "Ti Moune?" She affectionately used the title given to orphans who roamed the countryside. "Dreaming again? About what. Tell me."

Instead of answering, the peasant girl bowed her head and pretended to be absorbed in searching the dry earth for seeds, for bits of legumes they might have overlooked at another time. Her constant daydreaming, the way her eyes looked into space, upset her guardian. The peasant girl tried hard not to daydream when Mama Euralie was around her. Impossible. She sighed.

They worked in silence, raking through the dry earth, searching for carrots, turnips, sweet potatoes, or any addition to the small mounds of vegetables already culled to await the discerning eyes of road vendors. Puny? True. Dry? True. But during these hard times when peasants were reduced to eating only millet or cornbread cereal, even vegetables of poor quality were better than none at all.

Squinting from the glare of the midday sun, which reached through her thick, crisp hair to burn her scalp, the peasant girl walked with her toes curled away from the hot earth over to the bucket of water in the shade of a nearby tree. She dipped a gourdful and took it over to Mama Euralie. The old woman drank some. The peasant girl drank the rest. She took the gourd back to the bucket and stood looking at the tree leaves. They had curled from lack of moisture and awaited but one spark to go up in flames.

Oh, for rain. But a soft, gentle rainfall, not an angry storm of the kind that Agwe sometimes unleashed to devastate fields, flood roads, and sweep everything out to sea. That happened when, in his erratic behavior, Agwe chose to punish the ailing Asaka, blaming her laziness for all the ills visited on poor peasants. At these times, some believed that Agwe had gone mad.

Sighing again—for she often sighed—the peasant girl was turning away from the dry tree when a papillon lit on one of the curling leaves. Slowly she reached out her right hand. With her left hand she held to her shoulder an imaginary cage. Softly she put her hand around the butterfly. It fluttered in its enclosure. The peasant girl closed her eyes. Then, bringing the papillon to the cage on her shoulder, she opened her hand to release it. When she opened her eyes the butterfly had disappeared.

The old woman laughed. "If it's for rain you wish, pray the cage is not too crammed full of all your other wishes. Even so, force that papillon to squeeze in good. Rainfall this second will not be a second too soon—for me, for this earth, for your poor Tonton Julian." She wiped her parched mouth and turned to gaze warmly at the parting in the woods where the man and his mule had gone, heading toward the road.

The peasant girl blushed. She no longer knew what she had wished for. Had it been for rain? Or had her wish to do with the car that had just gone by? More and more her wishes, dreams—day and night—were tangled. She no longer knew where one began or the other ended.

It was the same when late that afternoon she walked through the woods on her way to the brook. She stopped to greet peasants still working the clearings behind their huts. She talked to them and listened, but once she had passed, she didn't remember a word that had been said.

When she came to the road, her mind became alert. She stood waiting for a car to go by. None did. Only camionettes bringing market people from marketplaces to their homes. Crossing the road, she kept on up the hill, stopping only when she came to the barbed wire fence that surrounded the Galimar estate. She looked through the fence at the men who worked for Monsieur Galimar from sunup to sundown. Most of the young men of the village worked for M. Galimar.

She stood studying them as they worked, digging into the rich earth of the fields that extended for miles and miles. They resembled carvings she had once seen in a marketplace—beautiful, mahogany brown skin stretched over broad backs, strongly muscled thighs and buttocks glistening with sweat through the openings of their tattered clothes, hats pulled low over their brows to protect their heads.

As the men dug, children romped, their bellies distended, plump, bare buttocks dusty from the rich soil of the fields, while mothers squatted between rows to gather the legumes that their menfolk unearthed, and which drivers of camionettes took into the markets in the big city.

Nor were these puny legumes. They were big, fat vegetables formed with the richness that moisture and good soil produced. On the Galimar estate, water was saved in giant tanks during rainy season, for use during the dry season or times of drought. But then, M. Galimar was a "grand homme."

Like most grands hommes, M. Galimar lived in a big city, far away from the lands that bore his name, and sent his children abroad to school. The peasant girl had heard that M. Galimar had a daughter her age, and that he sent her across the sea.

The girl had seen the great man once. One day on the road he had stopped his big, shining car to show off his land to his companions (tourists, it had been whispered). They had stopped for only a few minutes—long enough to attract dozens of peasants—then they had gone, flying off toward the grand ville.

How excited she had been! The look of the man, his car, his companions, had filled her with wild visions of unknown places.

She had asked Tonton Julian, "Are there no poor people living in the grand villes?"

"No poor!" the irascible man had bellowed. "If there were no poor, how do you think rich men would live?"

Despite Tonton Julian's scorn, the peasant girl had liked the gentle look of the tall, smooth-faced, tan-skinned mulatto with his straight hair. Many of the papillons she had captured and held since that day had had a vague wish attached: one day . . . one day . . .

Mama Euralie, always so concerned about what the peasant girl might be thinking, would often see the wistful way she looked at the productive fields of M. Galimar and mistake her longing for jealousy. "Ti Moune," she admonished, "there are many worse off than we, oui."

And that was true.

TWO

The water cascaded down the hillside into the brook and babbled around her, covering her body. It swirled around her feet, loosening the dirt packed between her toes and toenails—and it was good.

Working from sunup to sundown, seldom letting up to chitchat or rest, never stopping to pour a calabash full of water over her burning head, held a calculated reward. This.

While all the other tired peasants rested before going up to the hills to the Vaudun ceremony—to dance, to sing, to talk and rid themselves of burdens their errant gods had thrust upon them—the peasant girl slipped away and came here to nestle in this spot, just outside the Galimar lands.

Farther down, the water ran toward the river. Others went there to draw water for their huts or to wash clothes. But no one else ever came here to the brook. They obeyed a wordless command of M. Galimar, or feared his vicious overseer—or both. Only the peasant girl used the brook.

Protected by the woods of the hills and the distance from the road, she lay on the sandy bottom, letting water rush to thicken her hair and cool her head. The water massaged her neck, her body, her tired feet.

As she listened to the camionettes passing on the road, to the croaking frogs, the rasping crickets, and the hooting birds in the woods, she knew that nothing in the world could compare with the sweet softness of pure brook water. She passed her hands over her body, enjoying the feel of her skin.

She had the smoothest skin, the peasant girl. Black. Silk at the calves, satin on her thighs, changing to a velvet blackness as it spread up her shoulders, her neck, her face. The whites of her eyes sparkled and the black pupils shone like jewels. Villagers all agreed that Mama Euralie and Tonton Julian had come upon a most lovely Ti Moune.

She stretched out in the bubbling water and thought back to another time—a long time ago. She had lived in another village then, one near the sea. There, too, the village had become dry, then dryer from lack of rain. All the fruits had been picked from the trees, and Asaka, angered by Agwe's infidelity, had refused to nourish the earth. The seeds the peasants planted became seeds they were forced to eat. They had to abandon their village.

She, her mother, and sister had joined herdsmen who were moving west with their hungry cattle. Miles and miles they had walked, praying for rain. Cattlemen grumbled, "What have we done against Agwe? What have we done against the Almighty? It's our god-given right to have rain."

"It's so the gods do try us," another had said. "By the way we endure this trial shall they judge us."

So they had marched on that long journey, along that road parallel to the sea—the sea to their left, the hills, always the hills, to their right. The trees of the hillside mocked them, for they bore no fruit and their leaves, though curled and dried, were still green and clung to the branches.

And although the herdsmen had prayed, beseeching the gods, reasoning with Jesus, still it didn't rain. The girl, four years old then, the youngest, smallest, and weakest, had fallen. Her mother picked her up and carried her up a hill and put her in the curve of a mango tree.

That had been her orphanage, her torture, her nightmare. Loneliness had been her heritage—her mother walked away to rejoin the herdsmen, leaving her to die.

And Agwe roared.

A torrential rain fell. Water poured down from the heavens, raced through the bare mountains, and flooded the valleys with a vengeance. The sea, unleashed, rose in one great tide. It overturned the ships for miles out to sea, wrecking them. It capsized the boats of fishermen and dashed them onto the shores. It washed over the countryside, flooding the valley. It pounded the hills and threatened to engulf villages. But in one continuous wail the wind encircled the tree where the girl lay, and not a drop of water touched her. Then all was still.

And in that stillness, peasants from the surrounding villages emerged to search for survivors among the carcasses of cows and cadavers of herdsmen and peasants strewn along the road like refuse. They found none.

Mama Euralie and Tonton Julian had come down from a nearby hill. They had spied the peasant girl in the curve of the mango tree. Seeing her dry and unhurt, Mama Euralie had said, "Agwe must have claimed this child for his own. How else did she survive such a tempest?"

Tonton Julian, looking at the devastation around them, had cried, "Agwe? For whatever fiendish scheme can a mad god save a child? Indeed, that god has lost all godliness."

"Oh, Monsieur Julian," Mama Euralie had said. "Has there ever been an evil wind that hasn't in some way favored us peasants? If this is a scheme of Agwe's, then let us enjoy it. This precious Ti Moune must have been spared just for us."

"Another stomach to fill," Tonton Julian had grumbled, "for those of us whose mouths are forever dry." Nevertheless he had picked her up, gently, so that her head fell against his heart. Stomping knee-deep through mud, he had taken her back to their village, into the little mud hut with its thatched room, and put her down on what was forever to be her mat.

Désirée Dieu-Donné, they had named her—their god-given desire. Désirée loved her name. She loved the old couple. Never did she see them moving around the small hut, or plowing their land in the clearing in the woods, coaxing life back into the overused soil—the old woman forever hopeful, the old man forever disgruntled—that her heart didn't constrict with love.

Yet, as the years had pushed a childhood behind her, vague yearnings had sharpened a sense of her changing sixteen-year-old body. Mama Euralie's concern about her daydreaming added guilt to those unnamed cravings—an excitement for unknown pleasures, for racing, racing away in a car . . .

Désirée Dieu-Donné turned to lie on her stomach, and as she did she saw a papillon—blue and silver, startlingly lovely—winging on an overhanging branch. It actually gleamed in the last rays of the setting sun. Her heartbeat quickened, and after going through the rituals of making it captive, she felt a thrill quiver through her. She knew this wish, above all, had to come true.

Dusk fell. Silence settled. Insects rasped. Still she lay. She let the falling water woo her. She knew that Mama Euralie and Tonton Julian were having tea. She knew they waited for her, wanting to share this part of the day with her. Terrible child, why do you stay?

She lay, the churning water lifting, then lowering her, cradling her. Mama Euralie and Tonton Julian had finished tea and Mama Euralie was preparing to leave for the Vaudun ceremonies in the hill not too far from where she bathed. Dreamer, dreamer, why don't you go? Why are you waiting here?

Still Désirée lay—lilting, lilting, caught between the world of reality and her world of dreams. Darkness deepened. Silence, too. Camionettes that had been passing on the road with the consistency of overlapping waves diminished to an occasional few. Drumbeats sounded from the hills. The cacophony of insects grew deafening. They took over the evening. And you are still lying here? Insolent girl, for what are you waiting?

For what indeed? Désirée stretched out, loving the calm, the dark of evening. Only in this calm did the riotous change claiming her body seem real. Only then did she attempt to form a whole of the half-formed. The orphan whose meaning remained in the dim part of her mind—unresolved, mysterious, adding to the pleasure of a cherished innocence . . .

Night seeped down. Chanting, farther up in the hills, blended with drumbeats. Most of the villagers were up there at the ceremony. In this continuing drought, questions had to be asked of the gods—if the gods chose to listen. If the gods chose to possess the body of a believer and answer who was to blame for the peasants' plight, and why, and how.

Men like Tonton Julian were absent. They met instead outside of huts to talk, to complain, to drink rum and shout of their grievances to each other. Believers with battered faith, whose harsh lives had gone unrewarded on earth, they regarded with contempt the idea of a peaceful hereafter.

At last Désirée stood up. She stepped from the water to the bank, stretching up in the darkness as the water dripped from her tall, slim body. She reached for her dress on a nearby bush and pulled it over her head. When she did, she heard it tear at the armpits. She pulled it to her shoulders and felt and heard the tear widen. She pulled it on, but the tear kept widening, the rending sound getting louder, louder, louder. The ripping filled her ears, shutting out the noise of rampaging insects. Then came a resounding crash, so shattering that she knew a giant star had fallen to smash their tiny village. Then silence. A silence so profound that the insects held their breath. Beasts scurried to the safety of the underbrush and remained still—as still as she. Terror rose from her feet to her stomach, her head, paralyzing her—then forcing her on.

THREE

Timidly, Désirée began to tiptoe over dry, crumbled leaves. As she did, the creatures of the woods moved along with her. She reached out to touch first one tree and then another and another to guide her through the dark forest. Cautiously they went, Désirée and the creatures of the woods, gaining courage in the knowledge that they moved together. When they came to the edge of the woods, Désirée, still frightened, kept her body hidden in the protection of the forest. She stuck her head out and looked over the road. So did the chickens, squirrels, lizards, and other creatures that had come along with her.

But while fright held her to the shelter of the thick trees, curiosity forced them on. Désirée let the sounds of their scurrying feet guide her. She looked in the direction they were heading.

At first she saw nothing. Then she made out a silver glow in the dark. She drew back into the shadows, listening. But the twittering animals let out no shrill cries of fear or pain. Indeed, their excited chatter aroused her curiosity too. She looked out again. This time she searched along the road for people who usually sat out there chatting in quiet groups in the dark.

Where was everyone? Hadn't they heard? What if great harm had fallen from above to do them mischief? Did she have to sound the alarm? But the silver monster, glowing in the dark, remained still.

Désirée stepped out of the woods and crept close, closer. She drew near, nearer. Then, even in the dark, she recognized it. A car! Terror changed quickly to a thrill of expectation. She went up to the car and touched it. She, Désirée Dieu-Donné, touching a car! It was the first she had ever touched.

But this car had crashed head-on into a tree, and with such power that it had split the tree. The tree, in defense, had rammed in its front, forcing the fenders on both sides to hug the tree in desperation.

And as she stood, examining this strange phenomenon, she heard rasping breathing inside.

Désirée pushed her hand through the window. She felt somebody—warm, held against the seat by the steering wheel. A man, she knew from the feel of his chest. She moved her hand upward, from the wheel against his chest to his face, his head. A spurt of blood splashed warmly over her hand. She pulled it back. Poor man, hurt, but alive, sitting pinned inside the car, bleeding—perhaps to death.

She ran up the road, then back. She did not want to leave him alone. What if he died out there, in the dark, a stranger with no one to comfort him?

"Bon Dieu!" she cried out in the darkness. "A car is en panne. A man is in pain!"

Why? Why on this road, usually disquieted with the shuffle of feet, of whispered laughter, moanful sighs—like heartbeats forcing the dark to live—did no one appear? How, with so terrible a crash, did no one hear? Where were those who always knew of, or heard of, or sensed tragedy even before tragedy presented itself? Where were they all?

Once again Désirée reached through the window to touch the stranger, this time to comfort him, to let him know that he had no need to fear. She moved her hands gently over his face, his forehead, his hair. How soft his skin—like a girl's. His hair had the tex-

ROSA GUY

ture of silk. Gently she brushed it back, feeling the curls move beneath the touch of her fingers like little waves. Then his breathing stopped. Poor man, he was on his way. But at least he was not alone. She had been with him. And Désirée sang:

Dor, dor petit popée
You are not alone
I will guard you in your sleep
Over the mountains and over the deep
Until you arrive in safety
At the gates of Nan Guinée

As she sang, dozens of lamps appeared, dotting the dark night, some coming down from the hill, others approaching along the road. Peasants who had been hiding, listening, waiting to learn what new curse had crashed into their lives, met on the road and moved toward the car. She saw their lights coming, heard the shuffling of their feet, their sighs, their whispers: "It's a devil self, oui?" Or, "Who but a devil flies down a road like that, making poor folks scatter like fleas?" Or, "Flying, oui? As if the night belongs to him alone, as well as the day." And, "It's the way they do, these grands hommes. They forget that man is man, and beast is beast, and man and beast are entitled to life." And another: "What sins these grands hommes sin against us poor peasants! Their sins cannot be counted—or ever paid for. But Papa Gé caught this one in the act. He trapped him good—evil demon that he is." And still another: "Ah, oui, sometimes evil bestowed is justice given."

"But this man still breathes," someone said. "Papa Gé might have trapped him. But the Almighty didn't want him—yet."

So the angry peasants once again humbled themselves. They pried open the door of the car. They twisted the wheel from the driver's chest and lay the unconscious man gently on the ground. With the machetes they hacked branches from the fallen tree and made a pallet on which to carry him.

"Where shall we take him?" one man asked.

"To the cabin of Bienaimé, oui." And that was wise. Monsieur Bienaimé's stone house, built on a plateau in the hills, was large, sturdy, and protected from the excesses of weather.

But the injured man opened his eyes then. By the light of the lamps, the peasant girl looked down into them—strange eyes, gray eyes. How lovely against his bronze skin. A grand homme. Such a handsome grand homme.

"Take him to our hut!" she cried.

"To our hut?" Tonton Julian growled. "Where is there the room?"

"He can sleep on my mat," Désirée Dieu-Donné insisted.

"And you?"

"I have given my word to my loa, Agwe, while bathing in the brook this evening, and to the goddess Erzulie." She had added the goddess of love to make her case strong. If Tonton Julian didn't believe, the neighbors did.

"What? The gods were responsible for this crash?"

"Yes," Désirée said bravely. "I promised to care for this man, whenever he came—until he's well, or until his soul crosses over to the Nan Guinée."

And to her mind, where dreams and wishes overlapped, it was true. Or why had she captured the beautiful silver and blue papillon that had glowed in the setting sun, just as the car had glowed silver in the night? And why had she remained in the water—against her will? And why had she been the first to find him? And why had he crashed so near to where she was bathing? It had to be the will of her loa, Agwe.

Tonton Julian, seeing the fearful faces around him, the begging eyes of his little gem, shrugged. "When the heads and hearts of fools and children are filled with the images of gods and ghosts, what room is there for reason?"

The men carried the pallet to their hut. And it was the uncomplaining Mama Euralie who then objected.

"But, Monsieur Julian," she cried. "Rich men's sons must go to the big hospital for care. They must have soft beds on which to sleep, white sheets to cover them. What trouble have you brought down on our heads?"

"But who is he?" Tonton Julian asked. "We don't know his name, or where to find his father at this time of night."

And in the woods, made light by the dozens of lamps, the men and women stood discussing their problem around Mama Euralie's and Tonton Julian's hut.

No villager had ever seen him. Nor had they ever seen the car in which he had been driving through the dark like the devil gone wild.

And when M. Bienaimé was called for and had looked at him, he said, "I see no resemblance to any family I know." And M. Bienaimé, as a house builder, traveled all of the island and knew many people.

Someone suggested, "A stranger, perhaps? From Europe? From les Etats-Unis?" But M. Bienaimé shook his head. "He's a creole boy, to be sure. One of ours, from the look of him. But from what exact place? And of what family?" He shook his head.

"Perhaps this boy's been away at school," a man said.

"Ahhh," they agreed.

"And he is quite rich."

"Ahhh," they agreed.

And it was agreed that at dawn M. Bienaimé would go to the city in the direction the young man had been coming from, and M. Julian would travel to the big cities and towns in the direction that the hurt man had been heading. Then Madame Bonsanté, the healer, who grew herbs at the foot of the mountains, was sent for.

She directed the men to cut branches from the dry trees and make splints. She set the young man's broken arm and leg. She applied poultices to his chest to draw poisons from his wound. "It's the head we must worry about," she said. "The softness inside bruises easily and heals slowly—if at all."

She brewed teas to stop his bleeding from inside, and to clear his system of bruised blood. "If he's better in a day or so, all will be well. If not . . ." She shrugged. "Pray. We did what we know to do."

"Pray for me," M. Bienaimé said. "On the route I must take, the riverbeds are dry. If it rains before I get back, only God knows when I shall see my home again."

"I'll pray night and day for you to get back before the rains fill up those riverbeds, Monsieur Bienaimé," Mama Euralie said. Tonton Julian shook his head and laughed.

"Now we are asked to pray for the sun, when what we must have to survive is rain. It's in this way men participate in their own doom."

"True, true," M. Bienaimé agreed. "Misfortune never waits to be invited in. He comes to the door and takes off his hat, pretending he's welcome. He sits at your table and never leaves until he sees your bones."

Désirée Dieu-Donné heard the men talking outside the hut. She understood not one word. Curled up at the edge of what had been her mat, she gazed at the unconscious young stranger. And as she gazed she prayed, promising to keep a vigil over him as long as he needed—even if he needed her for life. Indeed, she had decided that the goddess Erzulie had asked this of her—and Agwe had demanded it.

ROSA GUY

FOUR

No one had expected the two men to find the house of the stranger in just one day. Nor were they worried when the men hadn't come back in two days. But then the third day passed, and the fourth. Villagers began to voice their concern: What if neither M. Bienaimé nor M. Julian found his home? What if this grand homme died in their little village? The police might come. The police were not known to be gentle with poor peasants. Days stretched. Five . . . six. Anxiety grew.

Not so with Désirée Dieu-Donné. She was anxious only about her young patient. She remained constant in her care. His slightest move brought her to his side. He grew feverish. She cut strips of cloth to bathe his brow. She made poultices for his chest and head. She forced tea past his teeth while cradling his head to her chest to guide the liquid down his throat. She rubbed his limbs with castor oil and massaged his arm and fingers to their tips, his leg to his toes. Indeed, her vagueness had disappeared.

Such devotion raised the fears of Mama Euralie. Young men were the threads from which daydreams were spun. But for that young orphan to dream of such a man? What nonsense spun around the head of Ti Moune?

"The stranger lies unconscious, Désirée," she complained after days of being silent. "He needs more rest and you need more work. Monsieur Bienaimé's place needs looking after."

Every day, Désirée rushed from the hut, through the woods, across the road, and up the hill to the housebuilder's stone cabin. She checked for animals or birds that might have strayed inside and nested. Then she rushed back, fearing that in her absence something might happen to her young patient.

One day she returned to find his splintered leg swollen and turning green. She dashed from the house to get Madame Bonsanté.

"Mon Dieu!" the healer said when she saw the leg. "What to do now? Even in big hospitals where they say miracles are worked men die of such wounds."

"He must not die!" Désirée cried.

"Pray," Mama Euralie said. "Pray hard. I fear more the revenge of the rich with their police than I fear the revenge of the gods. Better we had left him at the side of the road to perish."

The kind woman spoke from the strain of having her husband too long gone. What had happened to M. Julian? Had he found the young man's family? Had he gone to the police? What, then? Had the police thrown him in jail? Were they on their way here to punish the villagers? Old man that he was—after so long and hard a life—how much more did he have to bear?

Désirée Dieu-Donné's fears were only for her patient. His fever rose. His poisoned leg grew worse. Taking an old knife, she lanced the leg, drained the pus, and scalded the wound. She went to the brook and dug soap from the soap rocks at its side. She washed the leg and wrapped it with leaves that Madame Bonsanté had brought.

The old woman thought that the young man's illness threatened the sanity of the girl. "Ti Moune, there's work to be done. Only a rock is so blind as to guard only the earth on which it sits."

When Désirée did work, it was with reluctance. Then the old woman sent her away, saying, "What good are you, who I thought to be my helper in this old age? Go back to your young man if you must." And the girl stopped whatever she was doing and rushed to her patient.

One day she entered the hut to find that the man's eyes were open. He looked from her to stare around the mud hut. Then he closed his eyes in sleep. Did that mean the worst had passed? she asked herself. Did it mean he might live—get well?

The following day his eyes were open again when Désirée entered the hut. This time he recognized her, showed gladness to see her. She went to him, knelt beside him, and looked into his eyes. He tried to speak. The effort cost him pain. She put her fingers to his lips. His eyes smiled at her. Then he closed them and slept.

As M. Bienaimé had feared, the rains came. Suddenly. One moment the sun threatened all life in the village with its blistering rays. Then it went out. Low-hanging clouds brought instant night. Raindrops pounded leaves. Gusts of wind bent trees. The ground dampened, then was covered by a rush of water.

Praying in gratitude for the much-needed rain one instant, peasants abandoned prayers the next and went scurrying to save pots and pans being scattered over the ground. Chickens pecking in the spreading water gave up and ran squawking in fright. The wind strengthened. It tore the thatched roofs from huts and flung them into the air. In panic, parents snatched up babies and toddlers. Deserting their plots of land, they ran from the woods across the road and up into the hills. A few men, mindful of the stranger among them, rushed to the hut of Mama Euralie. They put the young man on the pallet and carried him up the hill, where they placed him on a mat in the sheltered stone house of M. Bienaimé. Désirée Dieu-Donné and Mama Euralie went with them.

The distant sea crested. Giant waves broke along its shore, overcame barriers of sand and forests, and rushed to meet the torrents of water pouring down through the bare mountains to flood the low-lying lands. Water rose with sickening rapidity. Mud huts dissolved and sank beneath the thickening currents. Trees were uprooted. Chickens, goats, pigs swirled beyond the reaching hands of owners. In minutes the peasants' possessions had disappeared beneath the rising water.

Rain fell in sheets. The wind raged. The onslaught of wind and rain tore off slats and crumbled the weak frame houses on the hillside. Needles of water drilling down into the earth softened it to mud. Houses and mud slid downhill, taking with them those who had been clinging to slippery rocks for support. In the muddy currents, some splashed around and grabbed shrubs or an outstretched hand to save themselves. Others sank to the bottom of the rising water.

Old women, children, and mothers with babies packed into the remaining sturdy houses. Men, younger women, and older children crouched outside houses, against trees and rocks, bracing themselves against the hard-hitting rain. And so it was all up and down the hillsides of this once lovely peasant village.

In M. Bienaimé's cabin, Mama Euralie moaned. "Monsieur Julian, where is he?" She rocked in despair. And when shrieks of terrified infants rose up in the cabin, she shouted in anger, "Dear Jesus, what have I done that my old age should guard only memories of despair! You gods!" She addressed them with uncharacteristic venom. "Spiteful Agwe, boastful Damballah, who claims to hold up the world, deceitful Erzulie, whose claim is to be the mother of love—in all my years of faith, why have you sought only to destroy me?"

Her words created a silence. They stilled even the cries of frightened babies. But outside the rain beat harder against the cabin, built to withstand the treachery of weather. Its stones threatened to give way and bury those sheltered within. Women pushed against the walls as though to give them support, while praying to the gods to disassociate them from the ravings of the distraught old woman, who had surely gone mad.

And so it was. Day seeped into day, night seeped into night. The distinction between day and night was lost in the hammering of the rain, the assault of the rampaging wind. The world had become water and mountains. The air was wet—even the air in the cabin. Water washed in through the door as some changed places to give respite to those in the punishing rain. Others went out to take care of needs—some as simple as filling empty bellies with rainwater.

Désirée Dieu-Donné used the rainwater to wash her patient's wounds. On the first day of the storm the young man had sunk into a deep unconsciousness. Then she had tried to keep his wounds dry. But as the air grew wet, then wetter, that had become impossible.

His fever heightened; his leg kept swelling beyond imagination. A smell of death invaded the cabin through his festering sores. Some left the shelter, choosing the pounding of the rain over the stench of certain death. Désirée Dieu-Donné sat at his side, washing his wounds. Wasn't rain the nectar of the gods? She kept repeating this to keep her hopes alive.

On the fourth day of the storm an old woman, weakened by the smell of rotting flesh, said, "What will happen to us if this pale, near-white youth should lose his limb? God forbid that he die."

"He must not die," Désirée said. "I shall not let him die."

"Blaspheme!" Mama Euralie cried. She had forgotten her tirade against the gods. "Who are you to question His will, Ti Moune? What loa entered your black body to give you the power to hold back death?"

Her guardian's anger silenced the peasant girl. But she looked down at the unconscious man and swore to him, in her heart, "I'll protect you. I'll do battle, if battle need be done—with the gods, even with my own Agwe, to keep you alive."

He shivered. She lay beside him and took him in her arms. He moaned. She bared her breasts and held his head to the soft warmth of her bosom.

ROSA GUY

Seeing this, the hysterical Mama Euralie cried, "What curse has been brought on the head of this wretched old woman? What disaster stalks this chaste child? She gives up honor to this man, born of a world as different from hers as land is from the sea. And haven't we seen these days what happens when land meets sea? What disorder? What disaster? Is it not better, then, that we be sucked down into these rising waters, to nourish another generation, than to suffer such shame!"

As the words came from her lips, the earth shook. Lightning zigzagged across the sky. Thunder—tons of iron rolling over clouds—threatened to join the rain and fall down on them. Wind swept the water into terrible waves that reached up to the hill and hit against the door of the cabin. Those inside buried their heads in arms, waiting . . . waiting . . .

Night came. In terror, they slept. All except Désirée Dieu-Donné.

She sat cradling the head of her patient, staring into the darkness as though she expected to make out a shape if she looked hard enough. She listened to the wind, the rain, and the thunder outside, alert for other sounds of danger. Inside, all was still. The silence lulled her, lulled her, lulled her . . .

Suddenly the shutters at the window flew open. To her watchful eyes, a shadow appeared against the outside darkness, a shadow that became thicker, larger, then formed itself into a man, a man in black who perched inside the window, his clothes as dark as the night behind him, his top hat outlined against the gray, stormy sky. Not a man—a demon! His mouth gleamed red, blood red. He grinned around a cigar clenched between brown teeth that were dripping with blood.

Désirée Dieu-Donné hugged her patient's hot body to her. The demon, still smiling, entered the window. Over the bowed heads of the sleeping peasants he hovered, then stood before her. Désirée thrust the sick man behind her. She leaped to her feet and faced the demon.

Papa Gé. She had never before seen him, this messenger of death. But she had heard of him, his evil powers. She knew of his persistence. The sense of evil he had brought permeated the cabin. She made her hands into claws and held them to his face to keep him at bay. Yet, knowing her helplessness against his great power, she cried out in anguish:

"Agwe, you who are responsible for my life. Erzulie, mother of love. Have mercy. Drive this demon of death from my sight. I swear I shall give my soul for the life and happiness of my love—my love!"

She spoke from her heart what she had known. She loved the young stranger. She had loved him since she had found him on the dark road.

At her cry, the face of evil grinned, then faded before her. The man disappeared. She looked at the window. The shutters were closed. Had the gods, then, accepted her vow?

Now as the storm raged, as the rain pounded against the shutters and on the rooftop, as the waters hurled by the wind beat at the cabin door, as thunder and lightning threatened the world, Désirée felt calm. She lay beside the young patient, cradled his body to her, and sang:

Dor, dor petit popée
You are not alone
I am here to guard you while you sleep
Over the mountains, and over the deep
I'll keep you here with me, in safety
Until you are well, or, ready
To leave for Nan Guinée . . .

FIVE

bird sang. The sun rose, a red ball in a clear blue sky. Those in the cabin raised their heads to listen. They looked out the window, then out the door at the miracle of morning. Then they joined the others gathering outside. They looked up at the mountains, where stone gleamed in the clear day. They looked at the woods, where standing trees supported those that had fallen, and knew that within that tangle of trees lay their future. They saw the waters rushing off, seeking outlets to the sea, and they laughed and shouted their victory.

Then one man said, "Look, the land is wasted, no food, no water. What to do?" Mama Euralie, her faith fully restored with the brightness of the day, saw only tomorrow's promise in the face of the sun.

ROSA GUY

"What storm is it that doesn't in some way favor us poor peasants?" she said, her eyes sparkling. The wrinkles on her black face were pressed out by a warm smile. "We know how harsh the sun has been, now feel how sweet it is."

Indeed, the peasants had no food and no tools; everything they possessed had been swept out to sea or was stuck beneath the receding water in the mud. But when the waters were gone, there would be the fallen trees with which to build, and leaves for roofs, and tools to rescue from the mud, and of course the mud itself . . .

"Every day is followed by night, and every night by day," Mama Euralie said. "After a time there's always another."

Désirée Dieu-Donné sensed the promise of new life in the heat touching her through the window. She looked at the man cradled in her arms. His eyes were open. For some moments eyes searched through eyes, then eyes smiled. They had won a victory over darkness, over death—they were one.

That day the men came. Peasants were huddled together, waiting for the water to recede, when a noise in the sky made them look up. They saw a big bird, a strange bird outlined against the clear blue sky. But Désirée knew it was no bird. It was a carrier— and it had come for him.

The carrier landed on a nearby plateau and was soon surrounded by dozens of wet, curious men who had never before seen a helicopter. The passengers who emerged from the big bird were city men dressed in rain slickers and hip boots. Slipping and sliding, they made their way over the mounds of mud, guided by anxious peasants pointing the way. They walked up to the cabin of M. Bienaimé and to Mama Euralie, who stood in the doorway. Then one man—a sad-eyed, smooth-skinned, bronze man with silver hair—said:

"Madame, I am Monsieur Gabriel Beauxhomme. I understand that my son Daniel Beauxhomme is to be found here."

"Mon Dieu, Monsieur le Patron!" Mama Euralie cried. "Is he your son, who flew out of the darkest of nights, on the roughest of roads, to crash into a tree with force that might have killed a dozen men? He lives, Monsieur. The Bon Dieu is kind. He gave him back his life, and my Ti Moune here cared for him— day and night."

M. Beauxhomme turned his gentle smile in the direction of the women grouped around Désirée.

Then he entered the cabin. Seeing his son lying wet and pale on the mat on the muddy floor, smelling the stench of his rotting flesh, the silver-haired father cried: "My son, my son, what have they done to you? Thank God you are not yet dead."

The men with M. Beauxhomme placed young Daniel on the stretcher. They carried him out of the cabin and, slipping and sliding, back to the waiting helicopter. Désirée and Mama Euralie followed.

Then M. Beauxhomme said to Mama Euralie, "Good woman, your man Julian is a good man. Intelligent. The directions he gave made it easy to find the way. Give him my thanks, and I leave him this." He handed Mama Euralie five gourdes. He climbed in and then they were off. The visit had taken less than ten minutes.

Désirée stood, her cotton dress torn beneath the armpits, her black skin exposed, the toes of her feet digging down into the mud. She looked up at the helicopter as it grew small, smaller, then disappeared. Unshed tears brightened her eyes. The sad-eyed man had not seen her. He had looked at the women looking at him. But he had not singled her out as different from the rest—she whose eyes surely bared her caring heart.

The gods had tried her. They had attempted to take young Daniel away from her. She had defied them. She had held him back from evil. She had laid his head against her protecting breasts and had breathed life back into him. The bird sang. Daniel had opened his eyes. Through their eyes they had sworn responsibility for each other.

Why, then, did the sad-eyed, gentle, sweet-faced man with his wise gray head not look into her eyes to see that she had to be with Daniel Beauxhomme, no matter where he went?

Tonton Julian returned seven days later. He came stepping through mud that reached his thighs. His shirt was torn to shreds and stuck to his dry, black skin in mud-hardened strips. He had lost his old hat, and his hair stood up white and thick on his head. A gray beard had grown on his chin. The villagers knew that M. Bienaimé was detained because of the swollen rivers, but they all had shared concern over Tonton Julian. "We thought the storm had done to you on the road what it has done to so many of ours," one old friend greeted him.

"Oh, it was hard," Tonton Julian said, as villagers gathered around to hear of his journey. "On the way I had no directions. No one knew of such a car. No one knew of such a man. And how to describe a man lying half-dead, a man who, when described, might be only one of many who live in the big city?

"But even the longest road must end. Only in the big city was it known that one Monsieur Beauxhomme had a missing son. Then I was directed to the house.

"House—a palace! Or it was once. Now a hotel. But what a hotel! It stands on a high hill and is surrounded by the Black Mountains. And what land— the hill is covered by the richest lands, which run like a river for miles.

"But when I arrived, I was barred entry. Three days I tried, and three days a guard—a brute of a man— stopped me. Only by chance did I happen to see the grand homme riding out of the gates. I ran after his car, shouting, 'Monsieur Beauxhomme, ton fils, ton fils.' God made him hear. He stopped. His driver backed up, and I told him. He was set to leave right then. But right then the storm struck. What a terrible time for us up there on that hill, never mind the protection of those Black Mountains. What a storm . . .

"On my way back, I lost my mule in a mudslide— on the first day."

"But Monsieur Julian," Mama Euralie fretted. "Why didn't you leave with Monsieur Beauxhomme?

It's been a week since he came and went."

"When did an ass accustomed to cushions care for one that knows only the jagged hardness of rocks?"

"He didn't ask you?" his wife asked. "And you gave him directions?"

"Mais oui. How was he to find the way?"

"Monsieur Julian, your tongue is not the sea, but one day it will drown you."

"What devastation along the road." The old man shook his head. "Here and there I had to stop to bury cadavers dug up from the mud."

"Ah, well, never mind," Mama Euralie said. "It's a bad storm that doesn't favor us peasants in some way. Monsieur Beauxhomme left you five gourdes." She showed him the crumpled bills.

"Then he repaid me with contempt," Tonton Julian said. "When a bare bone is thrown to a dog, it's to sharpen his teeth, not to fill his stomach."

"But now we can buy seeds, Monsieur Julian," Mama Euralie said, doing a small dance. "Our land will be rich. It will push out the biggest legumes." Then, looking from the grumpy old man to Désirée, standing before the hut forlorn and unhappy, she laughed. "Oh, Ti Moune, Tonton—how gracious the gods will be to us, you'll see."

SIX

With the irresistible urge of the tropics, life began again in that Jewel of the Antilles. The sun, finding the once-parched earth moist again, seduced it. Weeds, grass, plants jumped to life, painting the landscape a brilliant green. Seeds thought dead in the searing heat of the drought rejuvenated and pushed out fat legumes. Trees conspired with the sun to bring forth ripe fruits that hung heavy from their branches. Azaleas opened their faces. Poinsettias trampled to the ground by the heavy rains shook themselves upright. Eucalyptus and magnolia sucked away the heavy smell of rot, of death, cleansing the air. Peasants worked with renewed vigor, clearing dead branches from their plots and rebuilding homes.

Soon vendors dotted the roads again. Camionettes drove along the rain-gutted road, rocking with the loud laughter of a surviving people, while passengers recounted memories of the storm—that time when . . .

Désirée Dieu-Donné felt no joy in the awakening life around her. She saw the flowers, the plants spring out—scenes of brilliance to startle the eyes. She heard the happy talk, the ready laughter of peasants, but only one thought sustained her: I must leave.

But how? When? This is the way I must go, she told herself as she gazed down the road in the direction Tonton Julian had taken. How did one start? Put one foot out, the other is sure to follow, she told herself. But already Mama Euralie regarded her with suspicion. And that suspicion hovered over Désirée like a weight, depressing her, shackling her to the village. She loved Mama Euralie. How to defy her? How to tell her that she had to leave her and Tonton in their old age? The old woman held silent, but her bright eyes grew more anxious as time passed.

When they were alone, Désirée asked Tonton Julian, "Tell me again. How far is it to the home of Monsieur Beauxhomme?"

And the old man answered, "It's far, oui. Kilometers and kilometers. One must travel by the road as it runs along the forest. One must travel along the road as it runs by the sea. When the forest narrows to a point, and meets the sea, there is another road that crosses, leading east. One must take that road, into the grande ville—then one still has a long way to go."

And Désirée went to M. Bienconnu. He had lived long enough to see time chase time over and over again—and lived only to tell about it.

The girl sat beside him outside his hut and asked, "Monsieur Bienconnu, tell me about the family Beauxhomme. Who are they? From where do they come?"

The old man stared before him, looking back in time. "Beauxhomme? Beauxhomme? Surely a name given a child of a cherished concubine by an adoring father." He searched deeper into his mind. "Ahhh, oui. The grand homme of the Palace Beauxhomme, that mansion built on the hill in the protecting arms of the Black Mountains. Some say it's now a hotel."

"Oui, that's the one," Désirée cried.

"Gabriel Beauxhomme. He has but one son—studying in France."

"Daniel Beauxhomme is here, on this island," the

peasant girl said eagerly. "It was he who had the accident on the road before the great storm. It was he who shared the home of Mama Euralie and Tonton Julian. And Tonton Julian went all the way to the big city to find his father—Gabriel Beauxhomme."

"Gabriel Beauxhomme," the old man mused. "His father, too, was called Gabriel. The grandfather before him, now—he was Jean-Pierre Beauxhomme. It was the father before him that was called Armand—Jean-Pierre Armand. A French, he was—came to this island at the time of Napoleon. Poor man. But how rich he became—sugar cane, indigo, mahogany . . ." The old man gazed up to the tops of the denuded mountains and sighed.

"Now the story goes that this Frenchman built a lovely palace for his wife and children. He had, it is said, children like bush—all over the island—from concubines. But the house he built for the wife to whom he gave his name.

"Then he fell in love with a peasant girl—black as night, with skin as smooth as velvet, slanting eyes, and pretty white teeth. La Belle, they called her . . . Ti Moune," he said, studying the face of the peasant girl. "She must have looked much like you . . .

"Now this peasant girl had a child—a boy. So lovely,

his father called him Beaufils—at first. Then, as he grew older, naturally the name was changed to Beauxhomme.

"Then came our great war. Father and son fought on opposite sides. Son fought for the Revolution. Father fought for France and Napoleon.

"Ooh, the torment of the island—with fathers hating sons, sons hating fathers. Fathers killing sons, sons killing fathers—and brothers. And Beauxhomme? The Revolution decided his fate.

"The father was wounded and sailed for France. Whereupon the son claimed the castle as his rightful inheritance. He cast out the Armands—children of his father—and renamed the mansion. Castle Beauxhomme, he called it.

"Ahhh, but it was the father who had the last word with the curse he put on the head of his son."

"Curse?"

"A curse, oui. Never shall the Beauxhomme be free of France. Their eyes shall forever be staring across the sea."

"But the grand homme did have a peasant girl," Désirée Dieu-Donné said. She had heard only that part of the tale which pleased her. "Monsieur Bienconnu . . . I shall be going to the Castle Beauxhomme."

"What?" The old man looked down at the girl. "Have you said this to Mama Euralie?"

"Not yet," the peasant girl admitted.

"Tell her," M. Bienconnu said, "and heed her counsel. Mama Euralie has come through many great storms in this life."

"Monsieur Bienconnu, I know. But I now belong in the big city. Daniel Beauxhomme is there waiting—his heart is beating for me."

The old man shook his head. "Ma belle," he said gently, "To be tranquil, one must hang one's hat where one can reach it. Keep one's heart where one can feel its beat."

"You are saying that Daniel Beauxhomme cannot love me?" Désirée cried.

"Hélas, my child." The old man nodded. "History has cast our fate in stone."

Her fate! What nonsense. An orphan out of the storm, what did she have but dreams to sustain her? A future when . . . Such talk! The ravings of an old man.

Despite her annoyance, his words chilled her. She walked home in the late evening in panic. Her imagined shackles grew real. Her feet dragged. Occasionally she passed villagers threading their way through the woods toward the Vaudun ceremony in the hills, but she was too preoccupied to return their greetings. And when she came to the opening that led to the hut, she stood outside. The hut, the surrounding trees, the land had become her tomb. She had to leave. She had to leave now.

Tonton Julian was sharpening tools in the yard. He noticed her standing outside the clearing, and called to her. "Ti Moune, your face is troubled. What close friend has betrayed you?"

"It is I who am the culprit," Désirée exclaimed in desperation. She was relieved to find Tonton Julian alone. "I must leave this village, and I must go tonight. Now."

"Then someone did hurt you deeply," the old man said. "Come sit and tell your Tonton all about it."

"Young Daniel Beauxhomme is in danger. He needs me. I must go to him—or he might die." She went up to him.

"The road is hard for men and mules," Tonton Julian said. He held her chin and looked into her eyes. Anxious to leave before Mama Euralie arrived, she turned away. "It can be death for a little girl," he finished.

"I'm not a child, Tonton Julian," Désirée answered. "I'm sixteen years old—and strong. I have no fear."

"Ahhh, sixteen." The old man smiled. "That is the age." Then he shrugged. "But remember, bravery can sometimes be the mark of a fool, ma petite. The stronger the swimmer, the faster he drowns."

"Tonton, give me your blessing to leave and I'll be gone."

"What madness is this?" Mama Euralie appeared in the yard. "What is this nonsense I hear? Do my ears need cleaning?"

"I must go." Panic quivered Désirée's voice. "Daniel Beauxhomme needs me."

Mama Euralie pulled in her lips and stared at the girl. "A grand homme, so? Needs a poor peasant girl?"

Dusk had fallen. Worshipers passing by on their way to the Vaudun ceremonies heard Mama Euralie's angry outcry and paused.

"Agwe and Erzulie saved young Daniel from the hands of Papa Gé on the promise of my soul!" Désirée cried.

"Then it's the gods who have gone mad," the old woman shouted. "Monsieur Julian, I charge you—rid the child of this madness."

"What to do?" Tonton Julian said. "Our Ti Moune is sixteen." And seeing the determination in the girl's face, he added, "The chameleon is a small animal when it bites—until it hears thunder. If Ti Moune feels she must go . . ." He shook his head sadly.

"As hard as the chameleon bites at the sound of thunder, Monsieur Julian, remember it still must change color to survive."

A neighbor listening on the path said, "It's not only that they must change color, it's the way they must change—in the big city."

"Exactly," Mama Euralie agreed. Then to her husband she said, "Ti Moune is our treasure, Monsieur Julian. How do we get on without her?"

"My wife," he answered gently, "treasures that need constant watching have already been lost."

"But what joy can come from her hopeless dreams?" the old woman asked.

"Real joy only comes in the future," Tonton Julian answered teasingly, at which the old woman grew angry.

"With the best of intentions, careless tongues create disasters. Monsieur Julian, keep yours locked with its best friends—your teeth." Whereupon Tonton Julian gave a broad smile to reveal his stretch of gums and two remaining teeth.

"The best friendships can end through no fault of the tongue," he said. "In Ti Moune's case, it's the fault of the heart."

Seeing the old couple quarreling, Désirée made a move to leave the clearing. But Mama Euralie saw her ease away. She grabbed her hand, shouting to her husband, "We shall have no more talk of this until we consult the gods."

SEVEN

The old woman held the girl's hand tightly. She pulled her through the woods, across the road, and up into the hills. She had to talk to her gods—who sometimes acted foolish but were known to listen to reason.

Désirée stumbled on behind, her reluctant feet hitting raised roots of trees and tripping on loose rocks. She kept her mind on the old woman's hand. She had to tear hers away the instant it loosened.

Surefooted, Mama Euralie plowed through the darkening woods. She pulled, half-dragging Désirée along. She was anxious to make this most important plea to the gods. In all her nightly worship, she had asked only for simple things—a good harvest, clear days, strength for herself and the aging Tonton

Julian. They both wanted useful lives until death. They had always been satisfied with having enough to eat and drink, and with a sun and moon that remained faithful to the seasons. But this prayer for the mind and heart of a foolish girl might perhaps meddle in some fiendish scheme of a mad god. Her heartbeat quickened as they neared the houngfor. Still she held tightly to Désirée's hand, pulling, half-dragging her along.

Désirée kept her mind on the old woman's hand. The faint drumbeats grew louder. What if the gods decided to come on this night? What if they listened to Mama Euralie's plea on this night? What if, in gratitude to an old woman who had given them years of faith, they decided on this night that she, Désirée, had to stay? To stay? To risk her love, and perhaps Daniel's life, on a whim of the gods? She kept thinking of the hand holding hers, of the strong fingers.

From nearby she heard waterfalls. The cool freshness of the brook brushed her nostrils. The sound of the falling water and the sweet smell of the brook distracted Mama Euralie for one moment. Her hold slackened. Désirée snatched her hand away, and for seconds girl and woman struggled. But young strength is no match for old determina-

ROSA GUY

tion. Mama Euralie recaptured Désirée's hand and pulled her along.

Darkness deepened. The moon rose—big, full, its beams reaching through the trees to create shadows. Shadows danced among the trees. Shadows danced around them. Shadows snaked out to tease them. Shadows stood, sturdy as giants beneath trees, threatening. But the old woman feared no shadow. She feared but one thing—to lose Ti Moune. She strode through the fretwork of shadows, pulling, dragging the girl, and Désirée went stumbling along.

They walked into drumbeats.

Drumbeats reached out to them. Drumbeats went through them. Drumbeats filled their ears, their heads. Drumbeats wove them into the atmosphere, and suddenly Désirée grew passive. She submitted to the pull of the strong hand. Her reluctant feet slapped the ground in time. The beat became her rhythm, chilling, thrilling, forcing her hips to sway, her shoulders to move. The drum spoke of their coming. Drums picked up the reluctant beat of her feet. And when Mama Euralie and her Ti Moune broke into the clearing, villagers in the clearing broke into a chant:

Agwe, your child has come
Agwe, god of waters, of floods, of the sea
Agwe, who brought this errant child to be
Come guide her
Asaka, goddess of living things
Goddess of the trees, of the earth, of growing things
Come guide her
Damballah, Oueda, holding up this earth, the sky
Come guide her

The moon played tricks with the nearby trees. It flickered the shadows of leaves over the faces of the worshipers dancing and chanting in a circle. It made them seem faceless strangers. They danced their ever-expanding circle, moving first to the right, then changing to move to the left. They clapped their hands as they moved, raised their voices, and sang together, for it was good to be together, to dance together, to worship together, and—released from the grinding toil of the day—together to ask for small blessings. And on this night they had to ask for the release of an errant child from the crazy thoughts that had twisted her mind since she nursed a stranger.

The drums beating in her head affected Désirée. The villagers' singing and dancing together affected her. She wanted to join the circle. Orphan of the storm, found and brought here into the midst of these gentle people and sheltered by them, why did she want to leave?

Then she saw him. Leaning against a tree. He blended in with the shadows, but his head—the top hat, the cigar clenched in his bloody brown teeth, his gums and tongue gleaming blood-red—was clear in the moonlight. He turned and smiled at her. Désirée screamed.

No one heard. The drums kept on beating, the villagers kept on chanting, hands kept on clapping. Who was to hear her as Mama Euralie, thinking only of her needs, pulled her up to the dancers? They opened a space for them to pass—Mama Euralie and her Ti Moune. They walked through the circle, and dancers again opened a space for them to pass out.

Had no one seen? Or had it been a dream—a nightmare? Doubts arose. What if, on that stormy night, Agwe and Erzulie had not heard her plea? What if the smell of death, so strong inside M. Bienaimé's cabin that night, and the storm creating havoc outside, had conjured up a dream? If indeed she had only dreamed of seeing Papa Gé in that cabin, what then of Daniel Beauxhomme? Their searching eyes? Their silent vow? Had Mama Euralie already won? Did she belong here forever?

On the other side of the moving circle they approached the houngfor made of blankets draped over the branches of surrounding trees. Ti Moune and Mama Euralie stood outside the houngfor, and Mama Euralie called, "It is I, Mama Euralie, who wants to enter. I have talk for the gods—they who made a pact with my young innocent."

The silence from within was profound. Behind them circled the dancers, their steps livelier, their voices higher, the drumbeats gaining momentum. The flap of the houngfor lifted.

The room that the two entered was dark except for a candle on an altar and a lantern in one corner of the seemingly empty square. The light splashed their shadows over the crisscrossing branches above and the hard-packed earth beneath. Their shadows danced over the walls of the blankets to join other shadows poised about the enclosure but not yet seen. The candle flickered on the altar upon which stood a porcelain statue of the Virgin Mary, rosary beads draped over her fingers.

As Mama Euralie and Désirée Dieu-Donné adjusted their eyes to the dim light, they heard a voice: "My daughter . . . petite enfant whom I abandoned on the hill these years . . . oh, how I have missed you."

The hairs on Désirée's head bristled. Around her neck, cold fingers reached to still her shaking head. "Mama . . . ?" she whispered. She had answered to the call of that voice once. A well-remembered, cherished voice. A hated voice. A voice that indeed made of the moment a dream.

Désirée stared through the dimness to the altar at the side of the room. The Virgin stood cloaked in piety. How well she remembered the sadness of the voice, its pain. What bitter memories it evoked.

"It was for you, my child, that I left my village. It was for you I gave my life." The words had not come from the lips of the Virgin; they came from a shadowy figure standing beside the altar—a tall man, thin.

"I left you in the curve of that tree so that you might live, dearest daughter. And you have—thanks to this wonderful Mama—"

The voice stopped abruptly. The man crumpled to the ground, his body twitching. He lay there. The shadows poised on the blanket waited. Hands lifted him and carried him outside the houngfor.

The shaking inside her, the cold at her neck changed to an unbearable heat. Her heart beat from her chest to her knees. Oh, to awaken, to rid herself of this nightmare! Weakened, Désirée reached out her shaking hands. Mama Euralie took them. And the strength in those hands comforted Désirée.

Outside, the drums beat loud, louder. Fast, faster, the voices rose, building to a crescendo that stopped up ears with its density. Then all stopped. The gods had come.

In the silence, Désirée gazed around fearfully—fearing the silence, fearing the presence of the gods—any god. Fearing for her life, her sanity . . .

Then, from out of the dimness in the back, emerged a woman—tall, broad, beautiful. She approached Désirée, her white lace dress sparkling and heavy with beads. No such cloth existed in their village. No such woman.

Vain Erzulie. She chose only the loveliest women through whom to speak. And indeed, from wherever this woman had come, she was grand. "Black, beautiful Désirée Dieu-Donné," the woman said, smiling—a sudden slash of whiteness across her smooth brown face. "I am Erzulie, your loa of love," the woman said. "I do not hold you to the vow you made on that stressful night."

It had not been a dream! She had not imagined it! She had stood bravely between Papa Gé and her young patron. She had looked the evil demon in his eyes. She had clawed her fingers to his face. And this—this, too, was happening!

"Nor, ma belle," the goddess continued, "am I speaking of a most improbable love you hold for the young man—whose way of life is as impossible a distance from yours as the road you must travel to see him. What I shall speak of is love—yours for Mama Euralie—hers for you."

"How dare you!" The voice of a young man—brash-sounding, arrogant, yet as fresh as a gale of wind—had come from the lips of an old woman who sat with her knees to her chin in the darkest corner of the houngfor. She jumped to her feet and—despite her age, which had to be that of M. Bienconnu—pranced to the center of the room with amazing vigor. She faced Erzulie, her youthful eyes flashing with anger and mischief in the wrinkled face.

"Agwe, you here!" Erzulie cried with dismay.

"And why not?" Wrinkled lips leered. "What luck that I decided to come! Here you are, set—for whatever purpose—to undo plans that I have made! Who gave you the right to make a sham of promises sworn? I shall not be compromised. Do you hear!"

The last words were spoken in high, petulant tones, but the peasant girl warmed to her erratic god. His coming had put meaning back into her existence, her urgent need to run away and never turn back.

"Agwe, I pray you, let this unhappy child be. What designs do you have on her? You are already responsible for her mother's death."

"Punishment for lies," the brash voice corrected. "Did you hear her? She brought the child to the hill to save her? What distortion! It was I, Agwe, who saved the child. The woman grew weary, the child became a burden. Oh, but how they love to blame the gods for their weaknesses. They spend their lives on it." The old body, thin, emaciated, stalked the room, bright eyes snapping.

"Their weakness, Agwe?" Erzulie said, her anger rising. "The blameless peasants must carry the burden of your guilt? For the floods and destruction you cause?"

"Yes, yes. All those who support Asaka in her laziness."

"It's you who cause Asaka pain, Agwe," Erzulie said. "It's your rage that destroys her. It's your rage that erodes her power as you let this land slip bit by bit into the sea."

"No, Erzulie, it's they who destroy her." Agwe waved hands to include those within the houngfor and those crouched outside, listening, barely breathing for fear of sharing the stage with this most jealous god. And he made a grander gesture to include the world. "They and their greed," Agwe said. "They, they, they—and their so-called needs, the houses they must build, their ships, the statues that must be carved, the charcoal they have to burn. Oh, it is they who are thoughtless, Erzulie."

Gasps from villagers who had lost homes, lost lands, lost families in the most recent storm disquieted the atmosphere in the houngfor. Moans recalled to mind their suffering. Agwe spat: "Snivelers." All fell silent, giving back to him the respect due.

"Ahh, I shall destroy them, Erzulie. I shall destroy them all."

Peasants held their breath in a stillness meant to keep each blameless. And when Erzulie cried, "Agwe, you have gone mad!" sighs of agreement eased out, relieving burdened lungs. "Asaka was your lover, your sister, your friend."

"Erzulie," Agwe said. "Can you imagine a world where there are no bodies left for the love you try to project? How useless your wiles. Nor will I have a world where my wrath excites no fear, no dread, and my gentleness gives no hope. If there are no bodies, Erzulie, I have no power. But I shall not have my power eroded bit by bit, because of the weakness of lesser gods. Better I give Asaka the thrashing she deserves, push her into the sea—and destroy all . . . all . . ."

"Agwe, you are the most cruel of gods. The most selfish. The pity so much power had been given to you!"

"Should it have been given you, dear Erzulie?" Agwe mocked. Old hands went to provocatively moving hips.

Désirée watched them, their rage, their mockery, and pitied Mama Euralie her faith. These gods locked as they were in their world of power and vanity did not care about her, about the peasants. Désirée wanted to be gone. But Mama Euralie's hand held her, and the playacting of the gods held her fascinated.

"Love, love, love," Agwe taunted. "How they delight in the word. How they love the talk of dear, lovely Erzulie. Vain Erzulie—as though vanity were in itself a virtue. They create sweet verses about love to celebrate their immortal souls, while they destroy land and sea. Tell me, my well-meaning friend, do you believe that pride of the human body"—she

ROSA GUY

touched the sparkling white dress that adorned the goddess—"really saves the soul?"

The two gods stared at each other, anger matching anger. And those inside and outside the houngfor listened, knowing that at that moment nothing they said or thought or prayed for was of any importance. They waited, expecting the worst.

But with a sudden, wicked smile, the lips of the toothless mouth parted. "Erzulie," Agwe said, sweet, seductive. He snaked up to her so that they stood hip touching hip. "What we need is a grand romance. That is all that can save us—you, me, this Jewel of the Antilles. Love, chère goddess, but an all encompassing love. Let's force them to save themselves, and their immortal souls, through love."

"Force them? Or help them?" Erzulie asked.

"Do you think the islanders can truly love each other? The grands hommes—can they truly love us?"

"Love us?" Erzulie asked, puzzled.

"Yes, us—love you and me and Asaka . . ." He turned suddenly from Erzulie to grab hold of Désirée's chin. For one instant he gazed into her eyes. "And our great beauties."

"What if they can't?"

Désirée's lips parted to say that that had already

happened, that Daniel Beauxhomme loved her and she loved him.

But the restless Agwe had turned. The old woman flipped up her dress to expose her lean, tired buttocks, and sashayed away. Viewers gasped. They turned their eyes to the Virgin and made signs of the cross, refusing to be a party to even this god's rude behavior.

"Then I shall destroy them," Agwe snorted. He walked back and forth from shadow into light. "I shall destroy all. Then I shall use my wrath in the darkness and the light of a soulless world. I am a most powerful god, Erzulie. If I truly go mad, it shall be the end. We, after all, would have given them the chance to be responsible for each other."

"Ha, ha, ha." Mocking laughter drifted down, forcing eyes to turn upward. There among the leaves of the criss-crossing branches, Papa Gé sat, grinning down. "Even I shall lose my power at such a time," he said.

"Who sent for you?" Agwe's mood became ugly.

Papa Gé kept grinning. He floated down and stood before Agwe. "I came to make certain that vows given in trust be kept in trust," the evil demon said.

"What vows do you speak of?" Agwe demanded.

"Erzulie," Papa Gé said. But from the blank expression on the lovely woman's face, it was clear Erzulie had departed. "I wanted her to remind you—"

"I shall not have you here unless I send for you," Agwe shouted. "I shall not share this room with you." And the old woman sputtered, gasped, and fell lifeless to the ground, the last of her strength used up by Agwe's enormous energy.

"There must be room for me in all your plans," Papa Gé cried out to the departed god. Then he turned and gazed at Désirée.

The drumming outside started up in the wake of the departed gods. Low, deep, insistent drumbeats invaded the houngfor. In sorrow and in fear, villagers outside hummed and moaned deep in their throats as they always did when Papa Gé walked among them. And the candlelight on the altar flickered over the serene face of the Virgin, moving it to tears.

Then Papa Gé stepped over the frail, spent body of the old woman and walked toward Désirée. Désirée felt his hot breath fan her cheek. She screamed, snatched her hand away from Mama Euralie, and ran.

EIGHT

She ran for miles without once feeling the earth beneath her feet. Fear spurred her on, and desperation. She feared the all-seeing eyes of the gods. She feared friends and neighbors who might try to force her back. She had no wish to go back. Indeed, her way was before her.

Haunted, hunted, Désirée slipped from shadow to shadow, putting distance between herself and those who loved her, her home, her brook—her past. She took only her imaginary cage filled with papillons, her dreams; this she held to her—her future.

All that night she ran, ducking overhanging branches that came out at her through the dark. She dodged trees that suddenly appeared in her way. She slipped into ponds and crevices, and knew she had arrived at an unknown region. But only at dawn, when the shouts of vendors and the passing of camionettes on the road told her that she had followed Tonton Julian's unintended directions, did she slow to a walk. Yet she kept to the woods, still fearing the occasional familiar face.

The peasant girl walked on for miles. At midday, exhausted, she searched for and found a large tree, and curled beneath its sheltering branches. She did not fear the woods. The animals were her friends. They kept a respectful distance—as she did with them—but in times of danger, or with the approach of evil, they were sure to warn her.

She drifted off to sleep, her thoughts on the gods. What anger! Never before had she witnessed such behavior. How vain, how selfish, how proud and petty were these gods to whom the gentle peasants humbled themselves. How they scorned one another. And their ridiculous schemes . . .

The moment Désirée fell asleep, the gods grew to a size bigger than life in her dreams. Agwe—tall, beautiful, his lofty head of the richest blue-green seaweed decorated in gold—strutted back and forth as he had in the houngfor, his wicked eyes a blazing blue. Ah, the arrogance with which he threw back his head. But for whom did this selfish god care? Asaka sat sulking, looking drab and ragged in a brown dress. Erzulie, forever lovely, paraded herself so vainly. And all the while the gods preened, Papa Gé sat in the background with a smug smile on his mouth, his bloodied teeth clutching a cigar, and looked beyond Agwe and Erzulie and Asaka.

The peasant girl strained, but did not see the reason for his malevolent smile, the object of his satisfaction. She looked away, but the errant Agwe pointed. And following his pointing finger, Désirée looked upon Daniel Beauxhomme. He lay stretched out on a richly covered bed—sick unto death.

Désirée Dieu-Donné snatched herself awake. And it was night.

How far had she come? How far did she have to go? She walked from the woods to the road. Tonton Julian had said that the road to the Castle Beauxhomme was a long one indeed. One had to walk where woods ran parallel to the road. Then one walked where the road ran parallel to the sea. When woods and sea met and roads crossed, one kept north, then one still had a distance to go. Désirée had already traveled one night and a part of one day. Did she have much farther to go?

ROSA GUY

The road she came out on was like the one that went through her village. It ran along the woods on one side, with the opposite hills dotted by candlelight from frame houses or huts. At the foot of the hill, vendors sat along the road, their tiny candles stretching the darkness. Candles made the vendors seem faceless hulks crouching over their wooden crates. In the flickering candlelight, their whispers and soft laughter kept the night alive and busy.

Désirée walked up to the nearest vendor and asked, "Ma tante, can you tell me if this road leads to the castle of one Gabriel Beauxhomme who has a son, Daniel?" The woman shook her head, her face shrouded by night.

"Who is this Gabriel Beauxhomme?"

"He's a grand homme who lives in a palace on a hill, surrounded by the Black Mountains."

The woman turned to the vendor beside her. As she did, her profile shone in the candlelight—black skin as smooth as the few mangoes she had on her crate. "Do you know of a patron—one Gabriel Beauxhomme who lives near the Black Mountains?"

"No," the second woman said. "The Black Mountains? Papa, but that is far, oui?"

"How far?" Désirée asked.

"But it's long, yes? To get to the Black Mountains, you must first get to the big city," she said.

"I know," Désirée answered.

"And you're going to walk?" the first vendor asked.

"Yes."

"But why?"

"I have to see Monsieur Daniel, the son of Monsieur Gabriel Beauxhomme."

"But why?"

"He's very ill. He needs me," Désirée answered.

The two women turned to look at each other through the darkness. Then they pushed their heads out over their wooden crates. They looked first at Désirée's thick, uncombed hair and her ragged dress, then stretched out their necks to peer down at the peasant girl's feet. They laughed. Their laughter traveled down the road from vendor to vendor, so that at one moment laughter followed her, then soon laughter preceded her. Vendors left their crates to stand on the road to await her coming. "To the dreamer all things are possible," one vendor said. "Ti fille, go back to sleep, oui."

Désirée kept on walking. The laughter of the vendors confused and shamed her. But the road

ROSA GUY

was faster than the woods. And of what importance was their laughter when compared with her dear Daniel, lying near death at the Castle Beauxhomme?

Again she walked all night. By daybreak, once again she entered the woods, picked a wide tree, and curled up to go to sleep. But she hadn't slept long when a commotion awakened her. Going out to the road, she found it congested with morning camionettes arriving, unloading food, dry goods, and people, and driving off again.

Vendors of the day added their bulk and loud cries to those vendors who never seemed to sleep. Peasants walked through the crowds, holding indignantly squawking chickens by their feet. Butchers in bloody aprons stood over stalls, hacking freshly killed goats for customers. Young boys offered strings of recently caught fish. And everywhere townspeople were shopping, their baskets hanging over their arms. A town!

Indeed, not too far from the marketplace, Désirée saw rows of neat little houses sprawling over the countryside. Then it hadn't been so far; she had arrived. Going up to a woman who wore a pretty cotton dress and a head scarf of bright print, Désirée touched her arm. The woman pulled away as though from a beggar.

"Pardon, Madame," Désirée apologized. "But can you direct me to one Monsieur Gabriel Beauxhomme who has a son, Daniel?"

The woman twisted her shoulders up to better look down at the peasant girl. "How do you expect me to know such a person?" she asked.

"He lives in a palace on a hill, surrounded by the Black Mountains," Désirée said.

"The Black Mountains? But that's far, oui."

"But how far?" Désirée asked in distress.

The woman looked at Désirée, a cruel smile on her lips. "Are you riding?" she asked.

"No, Madame."

"Then why trouble yourself—or me? That trip will take away your strength and, if you get there, your youth." She walked away.

Désirée felt gloom descending. Fear and determination had brought her through these first two nights and days. How was it she still had so far to go?

She remembered Tonton Julian: "That road is hard for men and mules," he had said. "It might be death for a girl."

What if she lost her looks? She put both hands to

her face. Only then did she think of the gods. She had been so critical of them. So how to call on them for help?

Discouraged, but now knowing how long the road was, Désirée abandoned all thought of sleep. She walked through that day and well into the night. Then her strength failed. Finding a tree with wide-spreading branches, she curled up and went to sleep—and slept the clock around through the following night.

In the morning she awoke, well rested, her determination restored—and her appetite ravenous. Worse, the smell of grillot cooking on the road had seeped through the trees to tantalize her. Leaving the forest, she saw across the road a tall, heavy woman sitting bent over a big iron pot. Lanterns on both sides of her stand lit the surrounding road as bright as midday.

Overcome by hunger and the smell of the frying pork and plantains, Désirée walked over to the woman. "Mama," she said, "I'm hungry. For four days I have been traveling. I have had nothing but an occasional fruit to nourish my body."

"Why tell me?" the woman answered. "Troubles belong to us all. We choose the ones we court. My trouble is selling. Yours is buying. Both are about money. How much do you have?"

"Pas un sou," Désirée admitted.

"Not one cent?" the woman repeated. "That's the reason I sell grillot, my girl, and not sympathy. When my grillot is finished, I can rest my head easy."

Désirée stood looking at the stern profile the woman turned to her. Her aching stomach brought tears to her eyes. But when the woman refused to look back, she walked on. Then the woman called her back. "Ti Moune, give up easy, die easy, oui?" Taking a few pieces of the fried pork and some slices of fried plantains and hot pepper, she put them on a piece of old newspaper and handed it to the girl. "We peasants have survived on patience, mon chère," she said. "With patience we have learned to examine the bowels of a louse."

I have much to learn about patience, Mama," Désirée replied. "All these days I have traveled to get to the Black Mountains, in the grand ville. Now I have been told I still have many kilometers to go."

"That's for sure, oui," the woman said. "For that distance you will need a great deal of patience and more food to eat along the way." And she gave to Désirée many more pieces of fried pork and plantains.

Désirée thanked the woman and then went into the forest, found a soft spot beneath a tree, and ate

ROSA GUY

all the food the woman had given her. It didn't concern her that she might be hungry again. Her two nights of sleep had given her back her strength. The kindness of the woman had restored her faith. The gods must have forgiven her impatience with them. They were on her side. She had faith that Daniel Beauxhomme only awaited her coming to get well.

But the next days and nights brought her to a desolate spot, a long stretch of road gutted by too many storms and edged by a forest that had also been devastated. The fallen trees lay where they had toppled, and a thick junglelike growth claimed them. It took Désirée time and patience to come through this section. She knew of no detours. She chose the spots between road and woods carefully. Still she fell into big holes in the road, and in the woods, the tangle of the underbrush snarled around her ankles.

It took so much effort that by the time she was once again on the smooth road, she had become painfully hungry. She stopped at a grillot stand. This time she was determined not to ask the way. Each time she asked, the road seemed longer, her destination farther away. She looked down into the boiling pot of oil. The big woman behind the stand looked at her, then looked away. She was talking to a man friend. Désirée waited.

The woman looked at the hungry girl again, and kept on talking. Désirée waited. The woman kept her face turned from Désirée. Désirée kept on waiting. Finally the woman said, "But what is it with you?"

"Mama, I am exercising patience," Désirée answered.

"That's not what I sell here," the woman said. "Nor am I buying any."

"Mama, I'm hungry," Désirée said.

"Why didn't you say so?" the woman said. "What good is patience if not first accompanied by a wish?" Then she turned back to her companion and went on talking.

Now that her wish had been stated, Désirée waited, still silent. Finally the woman turned on her. "But, Ti Moune, what is it you want?"

"Some grillot," Désirée answered.

"But why didn't you say so?"

"I am exercising patience." Désirée answered.

"What for? All the grillot I had is gone."

The peasant girl kept looking into the pot of boiling oil. "I have traveled for six days. And in those six days I have eaten but once. It's a long way from my village and I still have a long way to go."

"And where are you going, may I ask?"

"I'm on my way to the Black Mountains, in the

ROSA GUY

grand ville," she replied. "Do you, by chance, know of one Monsieur Gabriel Beauxhomme?"

The question had been asked through habit. She hadn't meant to. But as she was turning away, the man friend said, "But who hasn't heard of Monsieur Beauxhomme? He lives on a hill in a big hotel . . . that is right. It is surrounded by the Black Mountains."

"Is it very far?" Désirée asked eagerly. Whatever this good man answered was to be a test of her endurance.

"Yes, it's far," the man answered. "But not so far. To walk from here takes no more than a day or so—three at the most."

"Tell me," Désirée asked, "is his son Daniel well?"

"He's rich," the man replied with a shrug. "If a rich man gets sick, he will be made well. If he can't be made well, he will die. But in his normal state, a rich man is better off than I."

Anxious once again to be gone, the peasant girl walked quickly away. The woman called her back. "Ti Moune, with all your patience and the long way you have to go, I'll give you bread—if not grillot."

NINE

Finally, on the seventh day, Désirée came to the place where forest and sea met, and where roads crossed. She was here. Never had she seen the sea so calm. She looked out over the water—the way it spread out, clear, turquoise, reflecting the sky. The sun sparkled it. In the distance the mountains looked down on it.

Désirée stared over the water, thinking of her long journey. She saw herself now—an orphan girl, alone in the woods, alone on the road. How had she arrived at this place of incredible beauty on this Jewel of the Antilles? Weary and happy, she sat on the raised root of a tree where earth met sand, and thanked Agwe for her safe arrival. She sank down and fell asleep.

When she awoke, the sun was descending in the sky and the water shimmered a brilliant pink. At the water's edge she saw a young girl stooping to collect things tossed up in the seaweeds.

"What are you doing?" Désirée asked.

"Searching for food," the girl answered. "I'm hungry."

"Where do you live?"

"I have no home," the child said.

"Have you no parents?" Désirée asked.

"No," the child answered. "My parents were taken away by the sea, in that storm which flew over the islands some months back. It took my sister and brother too. My mother had sent me to pick fruit on the hill. When the storm came, I ran for shelter in the trunk of a hollow tree. I had to stay there for days. When I got back . . ." The child's voice faded with a sigh.

At the child's answer, the guilt that had been hanging over Désirée since leaving the village lifted. Dear Agwe, he was not so ruthless after all. For surely it was he who had sent this lovely child to her.

"Ti Moune," the peasant girl said, "let me show you a road that leads to the nicest parents a child can have. But first, tell me, do you have a wishing cage?"

"No," the child said. "What does one do with a wishing cage?"

"One wishes, and protects one's dreams. One keeps the world open and the spirit free in a wishing cage," Désirée explained.

"How do I get such a cage?" the girl asked.

"Close your eyes and wish—hard. When you open them, it will be there. Orphans are always granted a wishing cage."

Then Désirée explained how to capture papillons and how to make a wish. "Must it always be a butterfly?" the girl asked.

"Always," the peasant girl replied. "The bigger and more beautiful, the better. So long as butterflies are free to fly from flower to bush and bush to flower, showing an equal regard to bush and flower, wishes will come true."

"And are they free to go when the wish comes true?"

"Yes, then you must release them so they may be free again to give hope for the future to someone else."

"Are all wishes sure to come true?" the child asked.

"That, Ti Moune, I shall have to learn," Désirée answered. Indeed, she had yet to have a dream come true. "But I have captured many—and I shall soon know."

"What if the butterfly is still on my shoulder when I open my eyes?" the girl asked. "What if it refuses to enter my cage?"

"Then it's not your dream. One person's dream might be another person's nightmare."

They searched but did not find any butterflies at the seashore. So the two orphans entered the woods and sat beneath a tree, waiting. Soon a butterfly alit on a nearby bush. The little girl rose. She moved quickly toward it and reached out her hand. The butterfly flew away. She looked at Désirée, her eyes wide with tears. "Why did it fear me?" she asked.

"Did you have a mean wish?" Désirée wanted to know.

"I—I just wished to wish . . ."

"But you must always know your wish," Désirée advised. "You must want that wish so that it comes through to the tips of your fingers. And while you are thinking of its beauty . . ." she moved her hands out slowly, whispering. "Oh, lovely, lovely butterfly, how wonderful that you were sent to grant this wish." Désirée smiled at the child. "Then as you ease your hands over it, so gently, it will wait. Your praise and wish will hold it still."

Once more they waited. They sat beneath the tree as the sun sank in the west and shadows deepened around them. They waited until it seemed the time for papillons had passed. But as they started to rise, a lovely papillon came to rest on the same bush.

This time the little girl moved slowly. She stood up and gently reached out her hand. The butterfly let her approach. It held still. Her hand closed over it. She shut her eyes and put the butterfly to her shoulder. She opened her eyes. Her first wish had been made.

"Don't tell me your wish," Désirée cautioned. "But now let me guide you. Walk through the forest until it runs parallel to the road. On the road there are always vendors—day and night. There are good vendors and there are vendors who are sometimes cross. But whether they are good or cross, always exercise patience.

"Your patience can often turn the most cross person into a person of kindness. So that if, at one time, one might not give you grillot, they will always give you bread.

"Sleep in the woods, for the trees and beasts of the forest are kind to orphans. But when you have traveled for four or five days, keep more to the road.

ROSA GUY

Inquire then, of all whom you meet, the whereabouts of Mama Euralie and Tonton Julian. Eventually you must meet someone who knows them and who will point the way to their hut.

"When you arrive, tell them that you were sent to them by none other than Désirée Dieu-Donné. Tell them your hopes of being their new Désirée Dieu-Donné. At that moment, Ti Moune, I know your first wish shall come true."

Désirée watched her go. When Ti Moune arrived at the old hut, one of Désirée's wishes would be granted too. She had always wished for Mama Euralie and Tonton Julian to be happy. She knew that her going had caused them unhappiness—and she had been unhappy too.

TEN

The peasant girl entered the city that same night. Even in the dark she sensed the vitality beating like a force. What excitement! Cars raced toward her. Headlights blinded her, forcing her into ditches. Warning horns alerted her to instant death. The occasional car she had gazed after with such longing back in the village had become an awesome reality by the dozens.

Between stretches of night and the glare of headlights, the peasant girl gazed in wonder at lights strung out, adorning roads like jewels. Through open windows she heard laughter. Loud music blasted, muting all sound.

Inching along, hugging the ditch, Désirée stretched tall to look into windows. She had to see the possessors of the laughter, the players of such lively music. And when she saw those heads thrown back in laughter, it seemed indeed to the peasant girl that they needed the world to laugh in.

She walked past houses where lights strung across spreading lawns revealed white-clothed tables set with an amazing array of foods. Bands played beneath trees. Men and women danced together, holding each other! A new world, a strange world. Women wore dresses of silks, satins, velvets, the finest cottons. In her deepest mind, the peasant girl had never imagined such fabrics. Such colors! They rivaled the colors of the island's flowers. And all wore shoes . . .

As she watched the resplendent women dancing in the arms of men, the peasant girl sensed a stirring within. Fear spread through her, up from the soles of her feet, through her body, her face, her head—an unnamed fear, never before felt.

She started to run. But this unnamed anxiety blinded her, and she tripped and fell facedown. Not on ground—on concrete, which did not yield to her weight. It bruised her face, the palms of her hands, her knees. More than the cars with their blinding lights, more than the music and the houses, this strange hardness caused her deeper unease. She who had traveled night and day with courage and confidence now suddenly succumbed to despair at the strangeness around her. Then an angry voice spoke out of the dark night:

"Ti Moune, the night has no eyes," it said. "If you walk in it, you must use yours, oui?"

Désirée had stumbled over the foot of a woman—one of a group who sat against the fence in the shade of a house, hidden by the night.

"Pardon, Mama," she said, scrambling quickly to her feet. "Please forgive."

But seeing the women sleeping in the shadows of houses gave her new courage. "Tomorrow I shall go on," she murmured. For the moment she was glad to draw comfort from the sleeping women. So, settling alongside them, she fell into a sound sleep.

At the first stirring of vendors, Désirée awoke, and in the dark of morning she went on her way. She walked, looking around at the grande ville and asking directions of those she met. The sun was already high in the sky when she came to the foot of the hill that had been pointed out to her as the one on which the Hotel Beauxhomme stood.

ROSA GUY

The hill curved upward steeply. Vendors with trays balanced on their heads formed a continual stream, coming down and going up on strong, muscular legs. Cars as impressive as that of M. Galimar forced them to the sides of the road. The peasant girl, joining the stream of vendors, started up the steep, winding climb.

She had gone halfway up when the road made a sweeping curve to reveal another hill across a deep void. There she saw the hotel. The massive building rose three stories and dominated the city that sprawled beneath. Nothing in her entire experience had prepared her for such an awesome sight—not even Tonton Julian's description. She had thought that to be the old man's exaggeration—a needed tale of one who had stayed too long.

The palace was grander than Tonton Julian or M. Bienconnu had words to describe. The structure was as wide as it was tall. Ornately designed it had splashes of gold in the white paint to catch the light of the sun. Balconies surrounded each of its floors. Doors opened onto the balconies.

Désirée hurried around the last few curves in the road. Approaching the hotel from the side, she saw the grounds of which Tonton Julian had spoken. Wide lawns in front were dotted with cultivated trees. In the back, lawns yielded to trees, giving the look of a thick forest. At the sides, the gardens were an assortment of bright flowers. All was fenced in by the gates that had been erected across the entire front of the hotel.

Désirée came to the front gate, which opened at the center, where the driveway led from the road to the entrance. Throngs of vendors clustered just outside the center gates—thick, impassable—waiting for patrons of the hotel to appear. Then they surrounded "les blancs," as thick as fleas, to hawk straw hats, straw baskets, fruits of every variety—bananas, mangoes, corosol, pineapples, coconuts—until the guests entered the gates, or until the vendors were chased by the two uniformed guards who opened the gates, quickly let in the guests, and closed them to stand guard inside.

Désirée Dieu-Donné studied that scene. How did one get in?

Then she saw that there were some vendors on the grounds. Artisans. They sat at the sides of the steps of the hotel entrance, displaying paintings, woodcarvings, sculptures, embroidered cloth. How did one get in there?

Put one foot out, the other will follow.

She walked boldly up to the milling crowd outside the gate and tried to push through. Unfriendly backs closed her out. "Pardon, Monsieur," she said to one man. The man didn't hear. She touched his shoulder. "Monsieur . . ." He looked around, saw her. With his elbow he pushed her away. "I did say pardon, mon frère," she said.

"But what do you want?" he asked.

"To get through," the peasant girl said.

The man scowled. He looked through to the front of the vendors. No one was selling. No one was buying. "You want to get mashed up in that crowd?" he asked.

"No, my brother. But I must get through the gate."

"What? You think your tongue can open locks? Go on, then." He let her through.

Then Désirée said to a woman blocking her way, "Mama, I must get through."

The woman squirmed around to see her better. "But get through to where?" she asked angrily.

"I must get through the gate."

"What are you selling?" the woman asked, seeing that she carried no tray.

"Nothing, Mama, but it's important that I get through."

"To do what? Lick the soles of those guards for a bone? Listen. Those two will swallow bones whole and choke themselves to their graves before they give a peasant a lick." But Désirée stood waiting. So the woman said, "Go on then, if you must, but it will gain you nothing."

The woman let her push on. Exercising patience with each vendor in turn, the girl worked her way to the gate. Then she called to the guards through the iron bars, "Bonjour Messieurs." The taller of the two—a big, broad-shouldered man with sweat shining on his black brows—turned, saw her, and turned away. "I say good morning, kind sir," Désirée repeated. The man kept his back turned to her.

Perhaps only vendors were prevented entrance? the girl pushed the gate open and squeezed through.

One step inside, and the other guard—a short, squat man with a thick neck—hissed, "Peasant pig. Get back with the scum where you belong." He lifted her in strong arms and threw her outside the gate, into the crowd. The other guard laughed.

Désirée shook in terror. The squat man's eyes, burning blood-red in his black face, seemed familiar to her, threatening. Seeing how she shook, one woman said, "But what do you think? You can just walk in so? Why do you think we stand out here?"

"I have come far. I have traveled many days and many nights to see Daniel Beauxhomme."

The woman pointed to her while shouting to the others, "Folle! Ti Moune here has come to see petit Beauxhomme."

"Papa, but that is mad," a man laughed. "What crazyhouse did she escape from?" Another pointed to Désirée's feet.

"The girl doesn't even have shoes," he cried. Then they bent over with sidesplitting laughter.

Désirée Dieu-Donné saw their shaking bodies and heard their laughter—derisive laughter that hit against her ears and pierced through her. At the same time a breeze blowing up the hill caressed her bare skin through her torn dress—her waist, her armpits. She looked down at her mud-caked feet, then at the feet of the vendors. They all wore shoes—plastic shoes, straw shoes, rubber thongs. Shame like a flame burned through her. She ran.

She ran down the hill, then through the city, retracing her steps of the day before. She ran until she found herself at the crossroads, once again where woods met sea. Exhausted, she sat on the raised root of the tree at the edge of the woods and stared out over the sea.

She sat for hours, not thinking, not understanding. Why had they laughed at her? Why had they hissed at her? Why had she been thrown from the grounds? She remembered her terror of the short man, and cleared her mind. She sat staring out at the sea.

By the time she started thinking again, the sun was setting and the water had already turned a bright pink. Then despair, the same as the night before, flooded her. Throwing her head back, she cried aloud in anguish, "Where can I get shoes?"

Just then her eye fell on a corosol on the branch of a tree overhead. And what a fruit! Even for a corosol it was big, heavy, its skin bursting with its sweet flesh and an abundance of juice. Désirée looked around, and finding a long stick, she pushed at the hanging branch. The corosol fell easily. She was hungry, but instead of eating the fruit she went out on the road again.

It wasn't long before she saw a vendor of plastic shoes. "Will you trade me shoes for this corosol?" she asked. The vendor took the fruit. He felt it, smelled it. "It's a fine fruit, to be sure," he said. "The finest corosol I have ever seen. But you must have escaped from the crazyhouse to think I'll exchange a pair of shoes that cost eight gourdes for one corosol that costs only two."

"I must have shoes," Désirée said in desperation. And she stood, determined to use patience if it took her all night.

The woman selling dresses at the next stall admired the fruit and took it from the vendor. She felt it and smelled it. "Ahh, but this is a lovely fruit, oui? Where did you get it, ma fille?"

Sensing that she might have further use of the tree, Désirée said, "That, my aunt, I cannot tell. The tree from which this fruit came was chosen by the gods."

"All the more reason I must have it," the woman said. "Will you take a dress for the fruit?"

"I must have shoes," Désirée insisted.

"It seems you need much more than shoes," the woman said, staring at the tear in the girl's dress, which went from her armpits to her waist.

The peasant girl laughed. "All things due me must come in their own time, my aunt," she said. "Now I must have shoes."

Désirée Dieu-Donné's laugh pleased the woman. She said, "But how is it that you are so black and beautiful, with skin of velvet, teeth of pearls, and hair so thick and wild as the wind—and yet wear such ragged clothes, have muddy feet and no shoes?"

"I have traveled many kilometers to get here," Désirée said. "So many days have I spent in the woods, I cannot count them. I came to find Daniel Beaux-homme of the Castle Beauxhomme. When I got there, the gatekeeper threw me from the grounds. The vendors laughed—because I have no shoes."

"This man who threw you—was he a dwarf? Neck thick from having carried bricks on his head for too many years? A cripple?"

"That's him," Désirée cried.

"Lucifus, that serpent," the woman spat.

"Peasant pig, he called me. He hates peasants. He called the vendors scum."

"Rotten teeth are strong only on rotten bananas," the woman said with a shrug.

"How frightened I was," Désirée said, recalling her terror.

"With reason, my girl. Lucifus is groundskeeper to the Castle Beauxhomme. He guards that world with his life, although he can never enter. Tell me, ma belle, why did you travel so far to see young Beauxhomme? It was madness, oui? He shall not receive you."

"I saved his life," Désirée said. "He had an accident in my village."

"Oui, I have heard of such an accident," the woman said.

"It was I who found him and cared for him. It was my Mama Euralie and Tonton Julian who housed him before the big storm."

"Ahh, oui, that storm which brought to us all our share of misery. How terrible it was. Those storms— they keep getting bigger and bigger."

"Then his father came and took him away."

"More dead than alive, I'm told. From what I hear, he's not long for this world."

"That's why I'm here," Désirée said. "The gods sent me. Agwe insisted that I come. Erzulie said the life I save is forever mine to care for."

Indeed, since running from the houngfor, the nights and days she'd spent sleeping in the woods had brought a profusion of dreams. Désirée no longer knew what was real and what imagined. She no longer knew if she ascribed to the gods words plucked from her dreams. She had come to believe her desires were the command of the gods.

"Erzulie speaks only truth. The life you save, like the infant you bear, is yours to care for—always." The good woman looked at the clothes of the girl before her. "It's also true that one cannot taste a fruit without first biting into it. It's equally true that one is not tempted to taste the prettiest fruit if it's covered in dung." Then to the shoe vendor she said, "The child is in the care of my loa, Erzulie. Give her shoes. I'll give you two gourdes and half of the corosol in payment—not a sou more."

The man looked at the peasant girl's feet. "Shoes?" he said. "Pray that I have a pair to fit those sprawling feet."

"The biggest you have will have to do," the woman said. And to Désirée: "Choose a dress from my stall. Blue becomes black skin. And take this . . ." She reached beneath her counter and brought forth the prettiest, reddest comb the peasant girl had ever seen. "A gift from Erzulie to me. Its teeth are big and strong. It understands the tangles of knotted hair. Its magic relaxes the hair and reveals the charm and beauty of the face beneath."

She handed Désirée the comb, warning her, "Even so, all might not go well—even with the help of gods. For the poor, all gates are difficult to enter—even the gates of heaven."

ELEVEN

For the rest of the evening and into the night, Désirée bathed in the moonlit sea. She washed her hair and combed the knots from it with the strong, big-toothed comb, gift of the goddess of love. She went to sleep and awoke the next morning with the sun. Then she slipped into her new blue dress and stuck the bright red comb in her hair. Never before had she felt lovely.

And indeed she was lovely, with her hair smoothed out by the magic comb and plaited in one thick braid that reached down her back. Her black skin, cleansed in the sea water and brightened by the blue dress, shone a deep velvet. Her eyes sparkled. Her teeth gleamed. All of this she saw reflected in the clear pools of water at the edge of the sea.

Confidence came. Her spirit soared. Then she put on the plastic shoes.

Désirée had never worn shoes. Her feet were large, her toes long, straight, and wide apart. These liberated toes she forced together to make them fit the confinement of the unyielding plastic of the too-small shoes.

What pain! Every step she took became a new experience in torture. Every step, as though from the turning of a screw, brought barbs of agony rushing from her crushed feet through her legs, her stomach, her heart.

But she had to have shoes to be allowed within the gates of the Castle Beauxhomme. She had to endure! She had not given up home and loved ones, had not traveled miles to be defeated by a pair of plastic shoes.

What courage it took! She dodged city traffic, running when she wanted to crawl. She walked tall when her body demanded that she bend. She refused the support of trees, of fences. Determined, she walked without once stopping until she came to the hill, where she pushed herself up and around its winding curves. Only when she turned the sharp curve that brought the hotel in view did her pain express itself in a single tear, which escaped a tear-filled eye to roll down a cheek.

At the top of the hill she walked slowly, deliberately, up to the vendors clustered around the gate entrance. She touched the first man and waited, expecting to hear a burst of derisive laughter when he turned. But upon seeing her, the man opened a way for her to pass, and it was so with the others, who parted like a fan, letting her through.

Then, as on the preceding day, she called to the guards. "Bonjour Messieurs." The tall man turned, and a big smile slashed across his massive face when he saw her. He started toward her. But at that moment a car leaving the grounds sounded its horn and he went to open the gates instead.

And as the driver of the car waited for the gates to open and for the guard to disperse the vendors, an occupant in the back seat looked out. Seeing her red comb flashing in the sun, the passenger said to his companion, "These ridiculous peasants. Did you ever see such a gaudy comb as the one that girl is wearing?"

Désirée did not understand what he said. He spoke French. She did recognize the voice—and the man. Monsieur Gabriel Beauxhomme. She ran to the car. At that same instant his companion looked out. Daniel Beauxhomme!

It all happened so quickly—as though in a dream. She smiled. It's he. It's he at last. She sighed. At last it's he. Her brilliant smile attracted young Daniel Beauxhomme, who said to her, "Mademoiselle, your face is not strange to me. Who are you? From where do I know you?"

He too spoke French. It didn't matter that she didn't understand his words. She said to him in Creole, "Monsieur Daniel, I have traveled far to see you. I am happy that I did. I see from your face, your eyes, that you need me. You are not well."

With impatience the elder Beauxhomme signaled the driver on. "Imbecile," he said. "How does one tolerate the insolence of peasants?" The car drove off.

Désirée still did not understand what the sad-eyed, sweet-looking old man had said. But she gained new confidence from the encounter—and finding herself inside the gates, she returned the smile of the smiling gatekeeper and walked boldly toward the steps of the entrance.

The gatekeeper had seen the exchange between the two young people, so he did not question her right to choose a seat among the artisans.

I shall never leave these grounds again, Désirée Dieu-Donné vowed, looking around her. I shall die before I do.

As though in answer to her silent vow, a papillon came to rest on an azalea bush beside the steps. Quickly Désirée captured it and put it into her cage. A nearby artisan, seeing her ritual, inquired what she had done. Désirée laughed gaily. Hearing her loud, happy laughter, all the artisans laughed along with her.

Hotel Beauxhomme was endowed with miles and miles of beautiful land. Fruit orchards spread out in forestlike starkness, brightened by a profusion of well-placed shrubs and flowers. Water fell down rocky slopes and into swimming pools that resembled natural brooks. Pheasants, guinea fowl, peacocks, and turkeys strutted around the woods and gardens. Rabbits and squirrels darted around, seeking shelter in the shrubs and the trees. This cultivated wilderness became the peasant girl's home. She had no other.

When Lucifus approached each evening, the artisans, aware of his hatred and jealousy of them and fearing his excesses, moved quickly to protect their works of art from his fury, his destructive hands. The end of each day brought confusion. This was the time the peasant girl slipped away. Then she spent hours, until his final rounds, keeping out of the groundskeeper's way.

Désirée Dieu-Donné lived in a sort of terror. But never had she lived so well. When darkness came, when guests gave up outdoor pleasures, when the night watchmen replaced those who worked days, the grounds became her playland. Then she kicked off her shoes, eased her sore feet in cool grass, and in the happiness brought her by the release from pain she ran and played freely.

In the orchards she gathered fruits. She ate them along with the leavings of guests' dinners, placed in buckets outside the kitchen for collectors. Meats she had never before tasted, buttered bread, legumes cooked in strange sauces became her nightly meals.

She bathed in swimming pools where bats swooped down to quench their thirst. She washed her clothes. She washed her hair and combed it with her magic comb. Stretching out at the side of the pool, as black as the night that absorbed her, she listened to the laughter of guests, to music playing, to the coming and going of cars, while gazing up at the windows of Daniel Beauxhomme's room. Only when his lights went out did she go to sleep.

For her place of rest, she had chosen one of the alcoves chiseled at the rocky base of the hotel, one directly beneath the rooms of Daniel Beauxhomme. There, protected from the night dew, the lights of the hotel, and Lucifus—for it was rumored he sometimes returned at night to spy on hotel workers—she snuggled down and slept soundly, awakening at the first touch of dawn. Then she quickly dressed, ready to outwit the ugly groundskeeper when he arrived in the early morning, until it was time once again to slip into her accepted place among the arriving artisans.

Never did she attempt to go into the hotel, or to try to see Daniel Beauxhomme. She longed to. But she feared being caught and banished from the grounds and losing forever her chance to save him. This forced her to exercise patience. The gods had sent her to him. She had to use her patience, until they sent him to her.

And they did.

In her sleep she heard him. Lying at the side of the pool, listening to the sounds from the hotel, she had drifted off to sleep. Suddenly she awoke. The hotel was still and in darkness, except for the lights in Daniel Beauxhomme's room and the sounds of footsteps coming toward her.

Lucifus? She slipped from the side of the pool and hid in some hedges. Footsteps came closer, closer, dragging. Limping? Through the hedges she saw a shadow outlined in the darkness—a tall figure, a man—slim, leaning as though on a cane. And as he came toward the pool, he looked a lonely shadow, forlorn. A terrible tenderness consumed her.

He reached the pool and disappeared. Désirée stood up and moved to the spot where she had seen him. She heard a groan. She kept searching until she sensed a hulking presence. It was he, kneeling with his head in his hands. She touched him and he groaned. She put an arm around his shoulder. He fell against her.

Then Désirée pulled his hands from his head, placed his head against her chest and sang:

Dor, dor petit popée
You are not alone
I've been sent to guard you
In your sleep, over the mountain
And over the deep.
I shall be here to comfort you
Until you are well, or until you
Depart to Nan Guinée

Over and over she sang. Over and over she caressed his head held against her chest, until his body slackened, until he relaxed in her arms, until out of the darkness, he spoke: "I have dreams." He spoke in Creole. "Terrible dreams. Dreams that plague me. Dreams of hands reaching out for me, of dungeons opening up to me . . . Then I feel that touch, hear that voice, that song . . . Your hands hold me back. Bon Dieu!" he cried. "I cannot stand those other hands reaching out to me. I am not so brave. I am not brave . . ."

"I'm here," the girl said. "I'm here to keep you safe."

"You are the peasant girl who stood at the gate," he said. "Who are you? Have I known you in another time? In another world? Your face . . . your voice . . . haunts me."

How sad. Sadness entered Désirée. It reached down into her—as deep as she was deep. Did he remember nothing of the days that had been so precious to her—days when she had begun to live, days that had changed her life and had brought her here, the wanderer, searching for him?

She spoke softly. "I am of this world."

"But it's impossible that I have known you—in this world." He laughed. He stood up, swaying. He might have fallen if she had not been there to support him. "I'm weak," he said. "So weak. Help me . . . help me . . . help me . . ."

Désirée slipped into her blue cotton dress and searched for her red comb. She put it in her hair. Slipping her arm around him, she helped him to his bed. He held on to her. She lay beside him, cradling his head to her chest. He fell asleep. She kept holding him, holding him, holding him . . .

TWELVE

ésirée awoke. Someone had shaken her. Her eyes went to the windows. Daylight. Never had she slept past the hushed stillness of dawn. She looked to the other side of her. A beautiful, dark mahogany-colored woman stood looking down at her. "Come, my girl," she said, placing a finger of secrecy to her lips. "It's time. You must be gone."

"I cannot go," Désirée said. She sat up. "I'm here to attend to the needs of Monsieur Daniel Beauxhomme."

"What insolence!" the woman said, drawing herself tall. "I am Madame Mathilde, Daniel's godmother and nursemaid. I take care of all his needs."

Tall, high-chested, her hair drawn severely back from her deep brown face, the woman had an enduring beauty. She appeared to be kind but firm, stern yet compassionate. She put a deliberate distance between herself and Désirée—the distance of the madame from the peasant. Yet in her demeanor was a quality that gave her comfort. And whatever the reason, she had accepted Désirée's presence in Daniel Beauxhomme's room and intended that they join in a conspiracy of silence.

"Madame, I cannot leave," Désirée said, touching the red comb to secure it. "I have been sent by the gods. I shall not leave until Monsieur Daniel is well."

"Of what gods do you speak?" the woman asked.

"The loa who watches over me is Agwe, god of waters," Désirée answered. "Erzulie, too, has given me her blessing."

A flicker of fear stirred in the woman's eyes. "Then the gods must be mad," she said. "If indeed your gods do exist. How dare they ask you to cross where there are no crossroads?"

"You question the wisdom of the gods, Madame?" Désirée asked.

"Tales of gods are told by men, not gods," the woman answered. "What care can you give to Monsieur Daniel that our great doctors have not already tried?"

"Healing comes from the heart as well as from the sage," Désirée answered. "Turn me out if you must. But by cutting off what's left of the bloom, will you not surely lose the fruit?"

The woman remained silent, hesitating. She had already questioned the gods. She did not want to challenge them. But by this time Daniel Beauxhomme had awakened and decided to join the argument.

"Mathilde, for the first time since my illness, I have slept an entire night and have awakened refreshed. This girl must stay."

"A peasant girl?" the woman asked, her voice expressing her distaste—and fear.

"A girl who has given me hope," Daniel Beauxhomme replied.

"What shall I say to your father? He shall go mad in his rage."

"Let that be my responsibility, chère madame," Daniel said.

The woman shuddered. She walked up and down the room, deeply agitated. "You are his one son, spoiled, used to having your way. He might forgive you this. But never shall he forgive me. How long do you expect this—girl to remain?"

"For as long as it takes, Mathilde," Daniel said.

And as he spoke, the door of the room opened, and the smooth-faced, sad-eyed man entered. He came into the room smiling, his handsome face open with the greetings of morning. Then he frowned, puzzled. He looked at Désirée Dieu-Donné, then at his son. Finally he turned to the woman who stood transfixed at the foot of the bed.

"Madame Mathilde," he said, "I beg you—what is this? What am I seeing? My son—in a tryst—with a peasant?"

"The girl claims healing powers given to her by the gods," Madame Mathilde answered. Whereupon the sad brown eyes widened in anger, the tan face darkened. Yet when he spoke, he cushioned his anger in a whisper.

"What nonsense." He looked at his son. "What do you have to say to such superstitions?"

"Mon Père," young Daniel said, then repeated what he had said before. "Last night I slept for the first time in a long time. I woke feeling refreshed. I must have this girl here with me."

"Mathilde." M. Beauxhomme turned his gaze to the woman without for an instant letting it rest on the unhappy girl standing beside his son. "I have trained you. I have talked to you. I have driven all

thoughts of heathen gods and their foolish ceremonies from your head. How is it that this morning
you speak like an ignorant peasant?"

"Monsieur le Patron," the woman said. "I raised
Daniel from a baby. I have known these months that
he must die. Yet he lingered. Now this girl has come.
And this morning I looked in his eyes and saw that
the shadows were gone. Is that not a good omen?"

"That, my dear woman," Gabriel Beauxhomme
said, making a sign of the cross, "is pure madness. It's
the teaching of the devil I hear coming from your lips."

"Monsieur Gabriel," the woman pleaded, "I have
listened to you. I have learned from you these many
years. But it is in the yard of the gods where my
umbilical cord is buried. Isn't the day-to-day learning
of one's lifetime the knowledge one must live by?"

"Madame, when one keeps learning that which
one has unlearned, then it's custom one worships,
not knowledge."

"Mon Patron," the woman cried, "I dare not challenge the gods! What if, when we throw out the
mud, we let the gold slip into the river? Will we then
not be to blame?

"Monsieur Gabriel," she begged. "Your son has
already been placed in the care of God by your doc-

tors. Can't we spare a short moment for the hands of this gentle child—before he departs?"

To this argument even Gabriel Beauxhomme had no answer. He stalked from the room without once looking back at the peasant girl sworn to save the life of his son.

Désirée Dieu-Donné felt a chill go through her, a foreboding. The sad-eyed man with his silver hair seemed unable to see her. He had looked at her on the hill in her village the day he collected his son—and he had not seen her then. She raised her hand to touch the red comb in her hair. As she did, she looked down into Daniel Beauxhomme's gray eyes. They smiled at her. Her heartbeat quickened. She smiled back. This, after all, was the reason she had traveled miles. This man was the cause of the hunger, the pain she had endured. She had walked onto the grounds and entered the palace it had seemed impossible for her to enter. She had come to make Daniel Beauxhomme well again, happy again. She had the gods on her side. What did it matter that Gabriel Beauxhomme refused to see her?

The work of Désirée Dieu-Donné—her heart's work, her life's work—began. And Madame

Mathilde worked along with her. When she wanted herbs, Madame Mathilde sent servants to fetch them from the Madame Bonsanté of the closest peasant village. When she needed teas brewed and poultices made, Madame Mathilde instructed the servants in the kitchen to prepare them. And it was she who brought them up to young Daniel's room, and helped prepare him for his daily bath. She stood by while the peasant girl massaged him.

What care! Désirée massaged his legs and feet to the tips of his toes, his arms and hands to the fingertips. She rubbed his back and shoulders with oils. She applied poultices to his crippled leg, which still held the earlier rot, and to his head. She forced him to drink teas to cleanse his blood, teas to calm him, teas to make him sleep. And she asked Madame Mathilde to prepare the potion of soup made up of blood, marrow, and bones, to give him strength.

And nights, when Madame Mathilde left them alone, Désirée curled up beside Daniel on the bed, listening to him breathe, ready to comfort him. When he cried out from his nightmares, she held his head against her breasts and sang:

Dor, dor petit popée
You are not alone
I am here to guard you in your sleep
Over the mountains, and over the deep
Through floods, famine, hunger and strife
I shall be here until you make me your wife.

And so her song had changed. Of course. This had been the wish of the gods. It had been her wish. To be with Daniel Beauxhomme, to make him well. To bring life back to him and to Asaka. To bring comfort and peace to Mama Euralie and Tonton Julian, and to peasants everywhere.

Ahh, the papillons grew restive. They beat against the cage. Had she not achieved her wishes? They wanted to be gone now. But Désirée Dieu-Donné held them captive still.

And in the days and weeks that followed, Daniel Beauxhomme grew strong, stronger. The peasant girl sensed it from his lessening weight on her shoulders when they strolled around the grounds in the evenings. In his room during the day, she saw it in his clearing gray eyes, and in the bronze returning to his pale skin. But more, she knew it through her own growing weakness.

She had poured her strength into him. She refused sleep, waiting for his moans. Relentlessly she fought the forces of night that threatened him, disturbing his sleep. Then one night, weakened from the battle, she moaned. He awakened. Finding himself in her arms, he drew her into his. She moaned again. He drew her closer still. Suddenly they were awake—alert. In each other's arms, tied there by an unexplained magic, giving to each other new delights.

Now their nights grew restless with the heat of a new need. Their days, cushioned by calm, held a new tenderness. They looked into each other's eyes and thrilled at the depth of their own beauty, a new knowledge of their own most secret selves. Indeed, they had fallen deeply in love.

They talked, and Désirée told Daniel of finding him on the road, crushed and near dead on that darkest of nights. She told him of the care she had taken, forcing him to live. She spoke of singing to him, and of how, in the calm after the storm, he had looked at her, and she at him, and how they had pledged themselves one to the other with their eyes.

Twilights, guarding their aloneness, they plunged into the deep woods. There, before the setting of the

sun, they discovered their love anew—in the unfold-
ing of buds into flowers, in the shrilling of birds to
their mates, in the movements of brilliantly colored
caterpillars, soon to become butterflies.

Désirée climbed trees and threw down fruits for
the crippled Daniel to catch. They ate them while
peering through crisscrossing branches at the sky,
seeing one star appear, then another and still another
until the world was but stars. They let waterfalls beat
on their bodies and swam in pools lit by moonlight.
They stretched out enfolded in each other's arms,
while in the dark, owls hooted overhead and chirping
insects questioned their wisdom in a low, throaty
chu-urp? Chu-urp? Chu-urp?

And the captive papillons, their mission fulfilled,
shook the cage, demanding to be free. But Désirée
Dieu-Donné held them captive still . . .

Madame Mathilde read the tale of love in the bright
eyes of the young couple. Troubled, she called Désirée
aside one day. "Ti Moune," she said. "The crisis for
young Daniel has passed. There's no longer need for
you to stay."

"But where shall I go?" Désirée demanded.

"I have no answer to give you. Monsieur Gabriel

has gone off to France. Whenever he returns, you can be sure he will reward you for his son's good health."

The woman's answer troubled Désirée, and confused her. She went to Daniel Beauxhomme. "Daniel," she said. "Madame Mathilde says you no longer need me. She wants me to leave. She said that your father will reward me for your good health. But how can he repay me for your health, when your life was mine to save?"

"There's no need for you to worry, my love," Daniel said to her. "You shall be with me always." When Madame Mathilde next came, he said, "Chère Mathilde, you have told Désirée she must leave. I say she cannot. I shall lose my health and strength if she ever leaves. And the next time I shall die. Désirée Dieu-Donné has earned my heart with her care. It now belongs to her."

"A curse," the good woman cried. "The gods have entrapped me! Monsieur Gabriel will punish me. You are my responsibility. As he left, he warned me to keep my eyes sharp and my senses alert. Oh, how I fear his anger."

"Madame Mathilde," the young man answered. "In this room Mistress Désirée Dieu-Donné is responsible for me. To you I give a new responsibility. Make my mistress into a grand demoiselle whom even my father will be unable to resist."

And so, the following weeks, the hotel was filled with excitement: dressmakers were hired, and hairdressers, and shoemakers. Beauticians and manicurists came and went. A buzzing, a gossip spread through the hotel and even into the grande ville. Everyone had heard about and was talking about the handsome Daniel Beauxhomme having chosen for himself a peasant as mistress.

Accomplished designers fashioned clothes and shoes of extraordinary beauty; their reputations in high circles demanded this. Lovely women, they made themselves ugly with jealousy; how did a black, a peasant, win the heart of Daniel Beauxhomme, a grand homme, whom they all desired? How did a peasant, a black, come to live in the Hotel Beauxhomme among the rich, whereas they, with their copper-colored or light tan or brown skin, and with all their accomplishments, had never been accepted but as highly paid courtesans?

As they fitted clothes on Désirée, or dressed her hair, these women kept up a stream of graceless remarks to each other, loud enough for Désirée's ears: "What do you think will happen when Andrea

Galimar comes back home from school in France?" Or, "I thought the Galimars and the Beauxhommes were to become one big family." Or, "I hear Andrea Galimar is more beautiful than ever. She always had the fairest skin—almost white." Or, "I hear that now Andrea is so-o-o polished." Or, "I wonder why Monsieur Gabriel Beauxhomme decided so suddenly to dash off to France?"

When Désirée had gone from the room the remarks were more direct: "My God, did you ever see anyone so black?" Or, "Does she really think she can hold on to that grand homme?" Or, "One thing Désirée Dieu-Donné will never have to face—a priest. Who ever heard of a rich mulatto marrying a black—rich or poor?" Or, "What a name, Dieu-Donné. God-given indeed! What God gave, God surely can take away."

Désirée and Daniel, insulated by their love, saw and heard only each other. After their evening walks and baths, they went into their rooms, where they looked out from the balconies. From one they admired the city sprawling beneath them; from another they looked out at the distant sea, calm in the moonlight as if waiting to display turbulence or gaiety or, as everyone knew, its overpowering savagery.

"I'm almost as strong as ever," Daniel Beaux-homme exclaimed one night as they looked out at the mountains surrounding the hill. "I have almost recovered my health and, except for my lame leg, my beauty. I thought I had lost both forever, and perhaps my life, in the wildness of my youth. How lucky I am that you exist, Désirée. How blessed to have you with me, child of the storm. Tell me, in this entire world, what can I give you?"

Désirée smiled. Happiness, she wanted to say. But she was already happier than ever. To be your wife, she wanted to say. But did that need to be said? Then she thought of Mama Euralie, or Tonton Julian. Looking up at the bare tops of the Black Mountains, she said, "There is an old man in my village, Monsieur Bienconnu. He says that once upon a time the mountains of this Jewel of the Antilles were green. He said they were thick with forests of hardwood trees reaching up to the sun. He said that a variety of bush and herbs grew among the trees, guarding their roots and supporting the goddess Asaka, who caused fertility and all growing things to live. Agwe respected Asaka then. He worked with her. Together they brought forth an abundance that protected the land and the people.

"I want those mountains green again. I want hardwood trees reaching for the sun again. I want them to work together to end misery on this Jewel of the Antilles."

As Daniel's arms tightened around her, Désirée looked down. In the shadows of the trees she saw a figure lurking. A man—a part of the darkness. He wore a top hat, and the cigar he smoked glowed in the dark. Désirée cried out.

"What is it?" Daniel Beauxhomme asked.

"There's someone in the garden. I'm afraid. It's someone who means us harm."

Daniel Beauxhomme rushed from the room. She saw him as he strode through the garden, searching. He came back a short time later. "No one is out in the gardens," he said, "except for that fellow Lucifus doing his rounds."

THIRTEEN

Gabriel Beauxhomme's stay in France extended for weeks. This gave his son time to prepare for his return. Désirée was now a lady whom all had to admire. He wanted his father and friends to agree. He planned a grand ball for the evening of his father's return. To the ball he invited the island's dignitaries, the wealthy patrons of the hotel, and the aristocracy of the island.

When the day arrived, the grand ballroom was expertly prepared by decorators. The floors were waxed to an incredible smoothness, the crystal chandeliers that adorned the room shone their brightest. The doors at the sides of the ballroom were opened to overlook the gardens, where lights hidden in the foliage brought the brilliance of the flowers into the

ROSA GUY

hall. Near the entrance of the hall, the band, on a raised platform and dressed in stiff formality, added to the elegance of the evening.

His plans went as well as intended. The ballroom was abuzz with excitement. Wine flowed. Music played as excited guests moved through the ballroom, meeting, greeting, toasting the return of Père Beauxhomme, until the gray-haired man was sufficiently drunk from wine and the pleasure of his warm welcome home. It was then that Daniel Beauxhomme chose to announce the presence of his mistress.

All fell silent and every eye was drawn to the top of the stairs, pulled there by a magnet: Mademoiselle Désirée Dieu-Donné.

Her dress of white satin contrasted sharply with her black skin, the satin adding a glow to the smoothness of her bare shoulders, a lushness to the velvet texture of her face. Her glowing hair had been pulled back into an elegant bun at the back of her head. Her shoes were delicate straps strung together to encompass her wide feet and covered with rhinestones. The couturières had indeed completed the magnificent work of art that nature had intended.

For a moment Désirée stood at the top of the stairs, looking down over the large ballroom crowded with more people than she had ever seen in one place. Then she descended into the speechlessness magnified by the music. The silence followed her down, then ruptured when, on the last step, she smiled to display her dazzling white teeth.

"Oh, most lovely," one diplomat, an African, said when he came up to her. "At one time thousands of our people were captured and brought to this island. Surely you are the descendant of our queen." A Chinese diplomat said, "Beauty such as yours is unreal. You must have been created by the most gifted artist, to be the legend of this Jewel of the Antilles." An Italian count knelt and kissed her feet, saying, "This is how I greet my Black Madonna." A German millionaire said to all who cared to listen, "I should tear my heart from my chest, if I had but one chance to win this lovely black pearl of the Antilles."

How strange! How wonderful! Désirée Dieu-Donné, who had never before been courted, floated from group to group as if in a dream. She did not speak, or understand, the languages being spoken. Forced into silence, she nevertheless understood the language in the eyes of her admirers. Her confidence soared, adding layers to her beauty. Laughter came easily, unmasking a graciousness that warmed the hearts of those who flocked around her, forcing them to create even grander praise.

The island's aristocracy, those to whom she might have spoken and whom she might have understood, drifted to one side of the room when Désirée stood at the other. She never noticed. Nor did she think it strange that whenever she smiled in his direction, M. Gabriel Beauxhomme happened to be smiling in another.

Her happiness lay in Daniel Beauxhomme's eyes! What joy shone there! What pride! Her life's pride. And seeing it, feeling it, added flattery to flattery. Her dreams were now a reality.

She danced. Because she had no words to thank her admirers, she danced for them. She danced for Daniel. And she danced for all who had made this night supreme, those who had given to her a new self-esteem. She danced to the beat of the drums. She danced to the chants of the musicians. And as chant and music gained momentum, she cast off her shoes, swaying to the drumbeats. She dipped, closed her eyes, and let the beat claim her, let it pull from her rhythms—rhythms of the Vaudun in the hills, rhythms of workers in the fields, rhythms of the waters bright in the sun surrounding the island. They flowed through her, these rhythms, adding grace to grace. Spectators gasped in awe at the spectacular performance of this most gracious lady.

Then, when the last beat sounded, Désirée bowed to them and smiled. Onlookers roared approval, crying, "Princess, Princess," and "Jewel of the Jewel of the Antilles."

Then Daniel claimed her. She walked off with him. No one had ever seen a couple so happy as the crippled Daniel Beauxhomme and the silent black beauty, Désirée Dieu-Donné, legend now.

In the weeks that followed, Désirée never saw the sly glances of the hotel maids, nor did she listen to the gossip about "the woman who took off her shoes." And it didn't matter to her that she was never asked to accompany Daniel and his father when le Père Beauxhomme insisted that his son visit old friends.

Désirée walked in a world cushioned by happiness, now that she had been received—even without her magic red comb. She had taken it from her hair at the insistence of her hairdressers and had thrown it into a drawer of her room. Now she went into the hotel dining room, smiling at guests who admired her for herself alone.

She dined on foods that, months before, she had picked from garbage buckets. She wore a different gown every day. No longer did she feel like Ti Moune, the orphan, the peasant. Now she was a lady of elegance. She awaited but one moment: the moment when Daniel Beauxhomme made her his wife.

And the papillons, maddened in their cage, demanded their freedom. But Désirée Dieu-Donné held them captive still.

Madame Mathilde, seeing that the young couple was blind in their passion and deaf in their happiness, grew distressed. When she saw how Désirée, reigning queen of the palace-hotel, was at ease in her new elegance, her distress grew.

"Désirée," the good woman said, "you have many suitors who want to marry you. Choose one and leave."

"The men are handsome. They are all kind. But I cannot leave Daniel," Désirée answered.

"Young Daniel is well. Your work here is done. Seek happiness elsewhere, while there is still time."

"Daniel is my happiness," Désirée said. "I am his. Madame Mathilde, I thought you loved him."

"I do."

"Then why don't you wish him well."

"I love him. And I love you," the good woman said. "And it's your happiness for which I am concerned. Your one chance for happiness is for you to leave now. Go as far away from this island as air and space will allow."

"I cannot leave this island, Madame Mathilde. I belong to this island, as Daniel belongs to it. The gods willed it so."

"Then the gods did curse you," the woman cried. "They know how deep the love of peasant and patron runs. How strong the bonds that bind them. But hatred runs deeper.

"We peasants hate them because they reject our blackness. They hate us because we remind them of theirs. My child, that is the curse of the Antilles, created by the enslavement of our fathers.

"Désirée Dieu-Donné, you are the best of us: woven from the fragments of orphans; imbued with the swollen hopes, the courage of dreamers; sensitized with the hearts of lovers; made compassionate through the tears of the poor, mourning those lives wasted for having lived. All have washed over you, deceiving you into believing that all things are possible. You are the best in us—our humanity.

"Oh, the gods did choose well. But how dared

they choose so tender a flower to bear the burden of our shared guilt!

"Go, dearest Désirée Dieu-Donné. Go, before this love destroys you—destroys us. Go now, my child. Go while this chance has been given to you— or, my dear, the ocean will not be big enough to hold our tears . . ."

Terrified by the woman's intensity, Désirée ran. She ran into the garden and stood looking around at the flowers, smelling their fragrance, seeing in the cultivation of the garden and the surrounding woods the accumulated rewards for her devotion. Then she cried out, "Daniel Beauxhomme and Désirée Dieu-Donné are one. All this belongs to us."

Then, in a frenzy, she went looking for still another papillon. She searched the gardens and the orchard. She had given up in despair when one alit next to her at the side of the pool. Patiently, Désirée reached out her arm. She was about to close her hand around it when a snarl from the other side of the pool forced her to turn.

Lucifus stood there. He kept staring at her, his ugly face twisted. Squat, massive of shoulders, he clenched and unclenched his hands. His red eyes reflected anger and hatred of this peasant-turned-lady.

He had heard about her, and resentment had kept him looking for her. Curiosity at never seeing her had fanned his resentment. Now he recognized her as the peasant girl who had sat with the artisans at the hotel entrance—elusive, untouchable.

And as he stood there, angry now that he recognized her, a change came over him. Désirée saw it. Papa Gé had taken possession of him. He became part of the darkness. His tongue darted from his hissing, blood-red mouth. He grinned around a cigar. Becoming agile, he jumped across the pool and reached for Désirée. But even though possessed, the groundskeeper found his arms shackled by Désirée's elegance. He dared not touch her. Instead he leered, spat, and was gone.

Désirée, her hand still outstretched, turned quickly to seize the papillon. But the butterfly sensed her terror and flew beyond reach. Overwhelmed by fear Désirée stood staring at the empty space where the papillon had been as though she had turned to stone.

ROSA GUY

FOURTEEN

On the night of Andrea Galimar's return from abroad, le Père Beauxhomme insisted that his son visit the Hotel Galimar with him to celebrate her homecoming. They left early. Then it grew late. From a balcony, Désirée Dieu-Donné looked down the winding road at cars driving up the hill, then passing through the hotel gates. The number of cars dwindled with the lateness of the hour to a few, then two, then an occasional one.

And as she stared out into the dark silence of early morning, all the hints and gossip dropped by dressmakers and maids for Désirée's ears she finally heard. It was as though, having been said, they had hung suspended in the air in bits and pieces, waiting for her mind to grasp. Désirée moved restlessly from that balcony to another. She stood looking down at the city, at the hundreds of lights stretching out into the darkness beneath her.

Then she understood. Those who held the destiny of the island in their hands were down there, beneath those lights beyond her reach. Those who held her happiness, those who had refused her speech at her ball—as surely as though they had stripped her mouth of tongue—were down in homes secure from her intrusion. And understanding this, she saw her terrible loneliness and cried out, "Agwe, Erzulie, have mercy, protect me!"

At her words a streak of lightning flashed across the clear sky. It lit the countryside as far as the sea, blotting out the city lights for one instant. Comforted, Désirée started to turn to enter her room, and then stopped. The lightning had also revealed the squat man standing in the garden below, looking up at her. And it seemed to Désirée that she had dreamed this before—an ancient dream—that things having changed nevertheless remained as they always were.

When Daniel finally came home, Désirée asked quietly, "Is it true, Daniel, that you and Andrea Galimar are promised to each other?"

"Since birth," he replied. "But we young people are no longer bound by the wishes of the old." Then he said, "Ahh, Désirée, what miracles travel brings. Our little Andrea has grown into a beauty. What poise! What grace! With her around, the Hotel Galimar has become a palace." He laughed long and loud, as though at the fond memories of a child who had surprised him with her growth.

Désirée laughed too. The strength of their love had been—and had to be—in sharing. She had shared his pain. Why not his joy? And this she did—even as her heart trembled in anxiety—in the weeks that followed.

Except for the limp of his once-infected leg, Daniel Beauxhomme had fully recovered. Days he went from the hotel with his father. Nights he returned home, flushed with happiness and lavish in his praise: "Andrea Galimar, how fast she runs. Faster than I when I had two good legs." Or, "What form! How well she swims—like a dolphin." Or, "You should see her sailing a boat. Désirée, Désirée, never have I seen such perfection." And each night, Désirée, delighting in his pleasure, vicariously enjoyed Andrea Galimar's perfection in things she herself had never dreamed of doing.

Not so Madame Mathilde. She looked at Daniel with averted eyes, and sometimes turned from him when he spoke. One day Désirée asked, "Madame, why are you so cross with Daniel? He is so happy. He's getting stronger every day—and so handsome. Were it not for his limp, he'd be the most perfect of men."

"The gods know well what they do, Désirée Dieu-Donné," Madame Mathilde admonished her. "The scars that twist the souls of men remain too often hidden beneath the masks of handsome faces. Monsieur Daniel will do well to remember the price he had to pay for his wildness—the pain, the misery and near-death—to gain manhood."

The time came when the Hotel Beauxhomme had to receive Mlle Andrea Galimar. Gabriel Beauxhomme took over the planning of the event. Invitations were printed and sent at the request of le Père Beauxhomme. The grounds of the hotel were decorated, lights strung, musicians hired, under the direction of the sad-eyed, gray-haired, handsome Père Beauxhomme. Foods were ordered and cooked under the supervision of the efficient Père Beauxhomme. When all was in readiness, it was left to le Fils Daniel, then to Madame Mathilde, to inform Désirée Dieu-Donné that she had not been invited.

From the balcony outside their rooms, Désirée sat

looking down at the grand reception. Longingly she listened to music being played. Wistfully she gazed at the richly decorated tables spread with the great assortment of foods. She searched among the guests— the island's aristocracy, who had stood at the sidelines of her reception but now were everywhere, laughing, greeting, complimenting each other. Then she saw the woman she had admired vicariously the previous days.

Andrea Galimar was easily the most perfect woman at the reception. Tall, white-skinned, with hair the texture of cornsilk, she moved from group to group in a long, golden gown, greeting each group in turn. And as she did, she spoke different tongues: German with the young millionaire, Italian with the count, French with the island guests, English with the African. Hearing her, Désirée, who had been forced into a numb, smiling silence when confronted with the same guests, felt a chill growing, growing inside. When Andrea Galimar laughed, it was a free laugh that needed the world to contain it.

Andrea and Daniel danced. They gazed into each other's eyes and talked. They laughed, their faces close. They moved to the music and then fell silent. Their arms tightened around each other and cheek touched cheek. They supported each other. He did not seem lame. They resembled each other. So much so that from the balcony they appeared to be two parts of one body.

Guests looking at the young couple smiled, whispered. And their whisperings, like hundreds of flies buzzing over a rotting cadaver, went to her heart. Désirée left the balcony.

In the room she stood looking at her own reflection in the mirror. And not understanding the reason for fear, she pushed her hands against her chest to still the flutter, flutter, flutter of her heart.

A shift of air spoke of the opening of doors. Then, there on the threshold stood Daniel Beauxhomme with his guest, Andrea Galimar. Désirée's and Andrea's eyes met through the mirror. Then Andrea said, "Daniel, how lovely. Never have I seen such a beautiful black girl. Can we keep her?"

Startled, Daniel Beauxhomme stared down at Andrea. She stared back at him. With the meeting of their eyes came the sudden knowledge in the room of their imminent betrothal.

That night, Désirée Dieu-Donné was removed from the rooms of Daniel Beauxhomme and put into a small room of her own at the far end of the hall.

FIFTEEN

Days passed. Désirée, in her little room, refused all food that Madame Mathilde brought to her. Sleep came only when her exhausted mind forced her eyes closed for the briefest moment. Then they opened again, alert, waiting for Daniel.

Days turned into a week, then two. She lost weight. Her eyes grew sunken. A weakness came over her. "Why is he not here?" she asked. "How can he treat me so?"

"Monsieur Daniel is away," the woman explained. "He has gone south. His father wished it that way."

"Then he hasn't deserted me," Désirée said.

"The strength of the hand is in the man's, not the boy's," Madame Mathilde answered. "Much like the rule of kingdoms is in the hands of kings and not princes. At that, you're lucky. What peasant girl can boast of such luck that the patron keeps her when he no longer has need for her?"

"What are you saying, Madame Mathilde?" Désirée cried. "I am Daniel and Daniel is Désirée."

"Stupid girl. The dirt at the bottom of our feet belongs to us alone. Yet water washes it away. Go, my child, while there is time. Cheat the gods. The African ambassador asks for you. The Italian count asks for you. Go, while light still fires your eyes and youth still quickens your body. Go before age claims you and the title 'Madame' becomes the ashes of your dreams.

"Let me comb your hair, change your clothes. Don't let those who would love you leave this island without you."

Désirée looked down at the dress she wore. She had not changed it since being moved to that room. She looked soiled, neglected. From lack of food she had lost weight and strength, and also the will to submit to the good woman's care. Her hair had lost its sheen and had knotted. Worse, her lovely red comb was missing—lost during the removal of her things from Daniel's room.

"Mademoiselle Andrea is lovely, Madame Mathilde," Désirée said. "But Daniel's admiration for her must pass. All will be as before."

"No, my child," Madame Mathilde said, shaking her head. "Monsieur Gabriel has announced the date of Monsieur Daniel's wedding to Andrea Galimar. The time is set."

"No, no!" Désirée cried. "That cannot be! It must not be!"

And Désirée waited for Daniel's return. He had to come back home. Day after day she listened at her door. And when it seemed that indeed he might stay away forever, one day she heard the shouts of servants, the blasting of a car horn. He had come back.

She listened to his limping steps on the stairs, heard the thumping of his cane on the rug as he reached the landing and walked to his rooms. His door opened and closed. She went in to him.

Entering his room, she saw him at the mirror, standing back at his own happiness. How beautiful, how incredibly beautiful those shining eyes, that face flushed from the sun and from an inner well-being.

"Daniel," she cried. "Tell me what have I done to give you displeasure?"

"Displeasure? You? You who found me, cared for

me, and gave me back my life? Never! It is this life that brings me joy. It is this life that I have pledged to Andrea Galimar."

When he spoke, his eyes gazed sadly out at Désirée. It was as though, having suffered greatly, he chose this time to tell the world that his had not been an easy life.

"Then must I leave?" Désirée asked.

"No, Ti Moune, stay. I love you. Andrea loves you. You must stay with me—with us—always."

That night Désirée huddled in a corner of her small room. A sudden shaking took possession of her body. She heard Erzulie's voice calling from the window. "Désirée, Désirée, you have lost your comb." Désirée touched her hair. "Why have you thrown away a gift of the gods, Désirée?" She shook her head as if to say she hadn't thrown the comb away. But it was true. In the days of her elegance she had thought little of her magic comb.

She turned to look at the brightness at the window. But it was not Erzulie who sat there.

"So young Beauxhomme saw no good in you," Erzulie's voice still spoke from Papa Gé's mouth. "And it's you who must pay."

A dream. A nightmare! Désirée tried to force herself awake. But her body refused to move. "Or he must pay."

Now the voice spoke brashly, in vanity, and with assurance. "Agwe saved his life on your most sacred vow—the promise of your soul. But, my chosen one, it was he who turned from you! So he must pay!"

One by one, the gods spoke through the mouth of Papa Gé. He sat grinning on the window's ledge, blood dripping from the corners of his mouth. In his hand he held out to her a shining blade. And Agwe's brash, angry voice commanded, "Here, take this knife. Strike hard, strike deep. Let his blood flow heavy. Let it run down the sides of mountains. Let it spread over the land. He has betrayed you—betrayed us all. Only then will we gods be assuaged."

Désirée forced herself to her feet, holding the wall for support, even while sleep held her fast. Sweat pushed through her pores, sticking her clothes to her. The shaking of her body increased. Her teeth rattled, her head hit against the wall. Then the bright light faded.

Désirée opened her eyes. She went to the window and looked out into the dark night. A dream? A dream, of course. She had known that even as she dreamed. Never before had the gods spoken through the mouth of that demon, Papa Gé.

She stood looking out into the dark night, feeling the dull ache, waiting for the ache to flare into pain as the nightmare quality left her and full consciousness returned. She stood until the first rays of sun lit the sky. Then rage seized her. How dared the sun rise as it had the day before, when the world had completely changed? How dared day dawn, when such tragedy had struck?

Daniel Beauxhomme had betrayed her! He had sworn to love her. Now he had pledged himself to Andrea Galimar.

Indeed, whoever had spoken those words, the truth had been said. She had saved Daniel Beauxhomme's life. Now his life was hers to take. As her anger rose, she saw beneath her window a knife gleaming.

Seizing it by its handle, Désirée left the room and walked barefoot down the long hall that separated her room from those of Daniel Beauxhomme. With a foot she pushed open his door and entered. Standing with her back to the door, she gazed around the apartment that a short time before she had thought to be theirs—for the rest of their lives.

Deliberately she moved to the bed and stood looking down at the sleeping man—the man who had spoken words so dear to her. Words so soon forgotten as to have been an exercise in passing the time. Was this why she had gone from her village? Was this man the reason she had run from Mama Euralie? The reason she had lost her beloved Tonton Julian?

Oh, that the world honored its pledges, she thought as she gazed down at his sleeping face. Oh, that the sun, the moon, the rain and wind honored their promised seasons. Oh, that men spoke only truth and those who built hopes in others only to let hope die should in the same way be punished. That was justice.

Daniel Beauxhomme lay on his back, his breathing deep and peaceful. She raised the knife high to plunge it into his chest. But, as though sensing her presence, he turned on the side toward her and smiled in his sleep. His handsome face was soft in the early-morning light. Shafts of tenderness pierced through to the deepest part of her. In confusion she let the knife fall from her hand. She ran. Ran down the steps, through the hotel, and out into the garden. At poolside she knelt and washed her face, rinsing the sleep from her eyes and cooling her tortured brow. She loved Daniel. He loved her. Whatever

Madame Mathilde said, before his marriage was consummated he had to remember.

And she might have killed him! At the thought of her dearest Daniel lying dead, she shuddered. No. Never!

"Peasant swine. Mother of a dog." Lucifus!

Then it seemed to Désirée that all that had happened—the dream, the knife, her going into Daniel's room—all had been a trick. Never had she intended to kill Daniel—nor had she been capable of it. All that had happened had lured her out here, into this garden, at this time of the morning, when it was inevitable that she meet this man.

"Filth of the earth!" Lucifus snarled. "You disgrace this place with your stench."

Désirée stumbled to her feet, but she had become so weakened that her knees buckled. She pitched forward. Lucifus caught her, picked her up in his thick-muscled arms, and took her to the gate. The gate-keeper opened it, and Lucifus threw her so she landed among the sleeping vendors a short distance away.

Désirée jumped to her feet and rushed to the gate. "Lucifus, Lucifus," she called. "I'm Mademoiselle Désirée Dieu-Donné, here by god-given right. You can't put me out."

Lucifus laughed. His laughter sounded and resounded through the grounds, down the valley, over the hills, and up to the Black Mountains. The mountains shook. Clouds gathered. Lightning flashed. The sun, which had begun to brighten the day, disappeared. Workers trudging up the hill shivered.

The peasant girl saw a waiter whom she had befriended at the gate and called to him, "Michel, Michel. I am Désirée Dieu-Donné, the peasant girl sent to care for Monsieur Daniel. Let me in."

The waiter looked at her strangely. "A likely story," he said. "That peasant girl is now a lady. And a very fine lady at that. With such a story, take care you're not caught and locked up in the crazyhouse."

The gatekeeper opened the gate for the waiter and Désirée forced her way in. But Lucifus was waiting. He grasped her arm and wrung it so that it came out of its socket, then pushed her back to the peasants.

"Tu folle?" one woman said to Désirée. "You must be crazy. Don't you know that for those such as us, it's licks to our tails for passing through that gate?"

"I am the mistress of Monsieur Daniel Beaux-homme," the girl cried. The vendors laughed long and loud.

"Ah, but you see she is crazy," the woman said. "Talk like that, my dear, will get you back where you came from—the crazyhouse."

"Listen to me," the peasant girl pleaded. "I was sent here by the gods to nurse Monsieur Daniel. To get him well again. Don't you see how strong and handsome he has become?"

And when the crowd might have laughed again, an old woman spoke out: "Let the girl speak. If it is the story of a folle girl, it is still a story we can relate."

And so Désirée told her tale to those vendors who chose to listen. When she had finished, the old woman said with a shrug, "Indeed, she might be speaking truth. Isn't it the pot that cooks the food which suffers the pain of the fire?"

And another added: "Hélas, oui. And when the food is done, who's barred from the table? That same pot. But what to do? Ti Moune, that's the way of the world."

SIXTEEN

The Hotel Beauxhomme grew busy and busier as the day of the wedding approached. Gardeners planted brilliant flowers, adding beauty to the already beautiful. Electricians strung lights intended to turn night into day. And with the hourly arrival of foodstuffs, the gatemen were kept busy opening and closing the gates all day long.

The skies grew dark and darker. Clouds hung low, then lower. They rumbled like the overstuffed stomach of a fat man on the day of a feast. Those who walked near the sea spoke of its being fresh, aggressive, its waves twitching impatiently. And one woman vendor said, "Pray those clouds lift before the wedding day. A bride needs sun to shine on her for her luck to keep that way."

When the wedding day dawned, the skies had again darkened. Thunder rolled like boulders hitting against clouds. Vendors sleeping at the sides of the road made fearful signs of the cross. "Ill luck for bride and groom, on such a day," a woman complained.

"Bride and groom?" another said. "And us? Isn't it we, the poor, who suffer most when Agwe goes wild? Pray he just threatens because he wants to frighten us, and not to destroy us. Haven't we had enough of his destruction?"

"Hélas," an old merchant said as he walked up the road. "What mischief to be done. The waves of the sea are giants, impatient to crest. Ahh, that Agwe, he has grown annoyed with us who are old and feeble, and wants to hurry us along. No more walking along with the years . . ."

The bright island flowers, their scents made strong in the heavy air, splashed loudly to force gaiety into the gloomy day. Waiters and ushers, stiff in white jackets and black bow ties, smiled and bowed their charm at arriving guests. Peasants brought in from surrounding villages jammed the road by the hundreds. Their musicians beat their drums. And the sounds of the drumbeats blended in with the rolling

ROSA GUY

thunder up in the mountains, echoed, and reechoed, then descended into the valley.

And Désirée sat among the vendors at the roadside. For two weeks she had not eaten. For two weeks she had not slept. For two weeks she had only stared through the gates of the bustling Hotel Beauxhomme at the mounting activity. Suffering the pain of her dislocated shoulder, she listened to the fears of the vendors. And seeing the fury of the gathering storm, she prayed, "Agwe, truth is not where the eyes can see. Daniel Beauxhomme's greatest love is for me."

At noon the church bells clanged. Cars from the hotel began a slow procession downhill. Laughing, shouting, dancing, peasants followed, sweeping Désirée along. They invaded the town, the townspeople joined in, and all flowed to its center.

Outside the church, Désirée, despite the pain of her dangling, useless arm, attempted to stand where Daniel might see and come to her. "Agwe," she kept praying. "Truth is not where the eyes can see. Daniel Beauxhomme's greatest love is for me."

Noise grew loud, louder, when Daniel Beauxhomme left his car and entered the church. It grew louder still with the arrival of the bride. Then silence prevailed as though revelers partook of the sacrament. Then cheers—long, loud, reaching up to mock the heavens. Daniel Beauxhomme had stepped from the church, with Andrea Galimar Beauxhomme on his arm.

A mistake! A mistake! Oh, what a terrible mistake!

The torture of her dangling arm increased with every heartbeat. Determined merrymakers guided her up the hill, back to the gates. She stood wedged among them, her face against the bars, looking in.

Foods had been laid out on long tables outside the gates. Foods had been laid out in the gardens inside the gates. Outside, peasants started the first feast for many years knowing it to be the last for many years to come. Inside, guests nibbled and chatted. Outside, drummers beat the drums of the island. Inside, musicians tuned up for the European music. Outside, peasants danced to the beat of island music. Inside, guests danced to the waltz. Food and rum were consumed outside. Liquors and foods were consumed on the inside.

Then the day lost its distinctiveness. Outside, dancers lost their servility. Inside, dancers lost intolerance. The island music and the island dance became the rhythm for all.

And during all the merrymaking, the thunder

growled like a dog straining toward an enemy. The peasant girl kept waiting for the miracle that seemed less and less likely. Then Madame Mathilde walked out of the hotel. She came down the steps. Désirée Dieu-Donné's heart leaped in expectation. The girl pushed a frail hand through the bars of the gate. With her waning strength, she waved. The good woman stood looking out at the teeming peasants. Her sad, searching eyes fell on Désirée. Then, with a sigh, she turned away.

"Madame Mathilde, it's me. It's me, Désirée," the peasant girl cried. But her voice, weakened from hunger and pain, was lost in the loud laughter and louder music.

Not long after, Daniel Beauxhomme limped up to the gate, his flushed, happy face bronzed and bearing the look of piety, his eyes sad despite their happiness. He threw out handfuls of coins, and the crowd fell to the ground, scrambling, snatching, grabbing. Daniel Beauxhomme looked out at them and laughed. Then his eyes fell on Désirée at the gate. Their eyes locked a moment, then he too turned and strode away.

He hadn't seen her! Just as his father, back on the rainswept hill long before, had gazed at her and not seen her, so too the son stared into her eyes with his sad eyes, and looked away.

The peasant girl glanced down at her mud-caked feet. She touched her ragged dress. She put her hands to her matted hair and cried out, "Where did I lose my lovely red comb?"

Thunder rocked the countryside. Peasants put their hands to their ears in an attempt to blot out the deafening sound. The peasant girl kept standing, her hand to her hair, her eyes staring at her muddy feet.

Then, from the crowd, "Here they come, merci à Dieu." Daniel Beauxhomme and his bride came out of the hotel and entered their limousine. "There they go," the happy crowd chanted. The gates opened, the limousine drove out.

In one surge, peasants surrounded the car, while others followed, sweeping Désirée along. "On to the honeymoon," one drunk shouted. Cheers went up. "On to life until death and hereafter."

Strong gusts of wind blew, whipping up the earth, flinging pebbles against the car. Excited peasants surrounded it, drunken peasants swarmed over it as if, indeed, they intended to accompany the young couple to the waiting ship.

Then policemen, who had been stationed unseen

ROSA GUY

for just such an occasion, appeared from the sides of the road. They swung their truncheons. The crowd fell back. The limousine sped on to its destination. Still, policemen kept pushing, kept swinging at the half-drunken peasants. In a frenzied scramble to get out of reach, the crowd pushed Désirée. She lost her footing. She fell. Weak from hunger and pain, she lacked the strength or will to pick herself up.

Then the policemen, whipped to unreasoning fury by the cringing crowd, hammered heads with their batons, and the fleeing peasants stampeded, trampling the girl underfoot.

Suddenly, swarms of papillons appeared on the hill. They winged over the crowd—big, beautiful butterflies hit against the heads, the mouths, the eyes of peasants, policemen, and guests. Thinking that to be a bad omen, peasants and policemen fled the hill. Guests quit the garden for the protection of the hotel. For a few seconds the papillons fluttered thickly over the body of the peasant girl lying on the road, and then they flew away. Only the corpse of the girl remained.

She lay unnoticed for some time. Then M. Gabriel Beauxhomme, on his way back from the honeymoon ship, saw the corpse on the road. He stopped his car and called to his groundskeeper. "Lucifus." And when the humble Lucifus came running up, he said, "I don't pay you good money to leave dead peasants in front of my hotel. Do you want to discourage my guests?" His sweet face was shining. His sad eyes were red from having shed too many tears over the successful completion of his son's wedding.

"Sorry, master," Lucifus said. "But you know how they are, Patron? They come, they fête, eat too much, drink too much, make damned nuisances of themselves, then haven't got the good sense to go when you tell them to." Picking up the corpse by an arm and a leg, he dumped it at the side of the road to await the garbage collectors. And Monsieur Gabriel's limousine drove on through the gate.

The promised storm broke with a vengeance. Its roar trembled the entire island. The first two drops of rain that fell, fell on the closed eyes of the little peasant girl. They resembled tears.

COLOPHON

My Love, My Love was designed at Coffee House Press
in the Warehouse District of downtown Minneapolis.
The text is set in Perpetua with Greymantle titles.

COFFEE HOUSE PRESS

Black Arts Movement Series

T HE POSTWAR 1920S was the decade of the "New Negro" and the Jazz Age "Harlem Renaissance," or first Black Renaissance of literary, visual, and performing arts. In the 1960s and 70s Vietnam War era a self-proclaimed "New Breed" generation of black artists and intellectuals orchestrated what they called the Black Arts Movement.

This energetic and highly self-conscious movement accompanied an explosion of urban black popular culture. The Coffee House Press Black Arts Movement Series is devoted to reprinting unavailable works of this period. We choose work that is masterful, that deserves another chance and other audiences, and that will help us keep the windows to the future open.

EDITORIAL PANEL Sandra Adell, *Associate Professor of Afro-American Studies, University of Wisconsin at Madison;* Alexs Pate, *Author, and Assistant Professor of Afro-American Studies, University of Minnesota;* John S. Wright, *Associate Professor of Afro-American Studies, and English, University of Minnesota.*

The Cotillion, JOHN OLIVER KILLENS

The Cotillion is a biting, uproarious satire that captures the conflicts between militants and social climbers within black society in the 1960s.

1-56689-119-1 • 5.5 X 8.5 • 220 PAGES • $14.95 • PAPER

Bird at My Window, ROSA GUY

Wade Williams wakes up in a mental hospital and is told he has assaulted his sister. As he retraces his steps during the course of the novel, the rich complexity of mid-twentieth-century Harlem and its problematic relationship to its residents is revealed in this powerful cultural critique.

1-56689-111-6 • 5.5 X 8.5 • 220 PAGES • $14.95 • PAPER

dem, WILLIAM MELVIN KELLEY

Upper middle-class Manhattanite Mitchell Pierce is convinced he has it made. With advancement at work, an attractive wife, and a comfortable apartment, he has achieved the sixties version of the white man's American dream. Slowly but surely that dream becomes a nightmare, and Mitchell can't seem to wake up.

1-56689-102-7 • 5.5 X 8.5 • 224 PAGES • $14.95 • PAPER

Captain Blackman, JOHN A. WILLIAMS

"Mr. Williams has written a provocative book in which fantasy and history merge and flow. His well-researched retelling of history is valuable, his novel fascinating reading and his message compelling."   —*The Baltimore Sun*

1-56689-096-0 • 5.5 X 8.5 • 288 PAGES • $15.95 • PAPER

Good books are brewing at coffeehousepress.org